a history
of
present illness

a history
of
present illness

ANNA DeFOREST

Little, Brown and Company
New York   Boston   London

Copyright © 2022 by Anna DeForest

Little, Brown and Company
Hachette Book Group
1290 Avenue of the Americas, New York, NY 10104
littlebrown.com

First Edition: August 2022

Little, Brown and Company is a division of Hachette Book Group, Inc. The Little, Brown name and logo are trademarks of Hachette Book Group, Inc.

Excerpt from "The Doctors" from *The Awful Rowing Toward God* by Anne Sexton. Copyright © 1975 by Loring Conant, Jr., Executor of the Estate. Reprinted by permission of Mariner Books, an imprint of HarperCollins Publishers.

Astonishments: Selected Poems of Anna Kamieńska, edited and translated by Graznyna Drabik and David Curzon. Copyright © 2007. Used by permission of Parachute Press.

ISBN 9780316381062
LCCN 2021945109

Printing 1, 2022

LSC-C

Printed in the United States of America

a history
of
present illness

Anatomy

All this happened, more or less. I have seen a beating heart in a wide-open chest. This place has been a miracle land. No one even dies until we let them.

I have a picture from the first day, the white-coat day. We all lined up and had little lab coats placed on our shoulders, our arms, by practicing physicians in doctoral robes. I struggled, I remember, to bend my arms back right, though there must be loads of people who know how to get a coat put on them. This was a sweltering day in the far part of summer when the rich leave the city and the poor flee into the margins, line the city's beaches in search of open air. At the service, the ceremony, faculty gave speeches, made cursory nods to the deeds we future doctors would perform for the good of society. But they were most

3

clear and constant and explicit about our suddenly obvious worth. Over and over, each of them said: You must be smart, so smart, or else you wouldn't be here. All of the other students had somehow known in advance to wear the school colors as a tie or a dress. So my clothes were all wrong, I can see looking back, as were my teeth, as was my hair. I look displaced and I am soaked in sweat. There is a sense, though, of light or life around the eyes—hope, almost? Now that I'm done, or close enough, I still have saved no lives myself, though I did check the pulse once of a woman who fainted on the subway. *Let go of me* is what she said.

We ended that first day by starting straight in with anatomy. They had us change into scrubs in a large conference room next to the cadaver lab divided by a rolling wall between the women and the men. I tried to keep my eyes on the floor. Four students were assigned to each table, each with a body facedown and draped in terry cloth soaked in phenol and glycerin. Ours was an elderly Black woman, almost gray, in size and shape so much like a West Indian neighbor I'd had before I came here who kept a barrel in the hall for all the goods she collected to send home monthly on a freighter. She lived with her brother, a gangly man who collected bottles and cans, who smoked in the stairwell and drummed on the walls to music playing only in his head.

The anatomy group was two women and two men. If you looked around the room you could see the groups were for the most part arranged this way, with some rare imbalance—the gender skew in medical school had recently turned slightly toward women. My group was an even split. One of the men was tall, white, with a tan, built but not quite well enough to counter his childlike face. For some reason he mentioned right away that he had a country house nearby to stay in on the weekends. The other man was from Texas. He said that whenever he said that, on interviews or wherever, they would next ask him where his parents were from, because of his name, apparently, or the color of his skin. He certainly did not have an accent. We all wore masks, which made faces hard to read, but made it, I found, easier to sustain eye contact. The other woman stood near the textbook, which was under a sheet of plastic to protect it from the fluids that quickly came to coat our gloved hands, and read out instructions to the rest of us.

Where did the bodies come from? I assumed they volunteered, though of course it would be difficult to recruit for such demand, to find enough people perimortem so committed to medical education. A fourth-year who used to write death notices for a national newspaper rounded up a group of us to write obituaries for some of the cadavers. After learning the basic technique, we would meet with the families or speak to them on the phone. I wanted to be assigned my own body's family, but this was ruled out by the study's design. Everything we did was studied, written up, and published in peer-reviewed journals. The whole school was rich with projects to prove that doctors could be made humane. So I was assigned some other group's cadaver. His wife told me that she planned to become one too. For science, she said, and the savings they gave you on burial.

The country-house man took the first turn with the scalpel and drew a long line down our body's back, and then we took turns pulling the skin away from the fat and fascia with knives and little scissors. She had wide shoulders and thin arms and was unnaturally flat from settling in the fixative. Her face and hands were wrapped in black plastic to keep them from drying out. It is normal from what I have read to have some feeling for your cadaver, though only the students who are women ever seemed to admit this. But the body was a problem right away for the country-house man. Once the spine was exposed, we had to crack each vertebra with a chisel and a hammer, slowly revealing the spinal cord. Fuck, this man said. Goddamn it, as the chisel slipped again. I had to imagine he was disappointed to be making such a bad job of her. Don't swear, I said, and he did stop, though it was his high-stakes disposition that later passed us through every test. I was the weak link from the beginning. I have never had much skill at or interest in learning just the names for things. Once I came to the lab alone to attempt remediation, trying to learn the nerves of her neck. I even cut her ear off to clear the field, but it was useless. I was distracted, alone in the lab. Of thirty-one bodies, the only one who wasn't dead.

But I was right about the volume. The lack of donor bodies was made up in unclaimed remains. The indigent or chronically isolated, so common in the city, even nursing-home residents, done now languishing in dementia, who had saved for a nice single grave in a field somewhere, but the money got lost or diverted somehow, so they ended up here on these tables with their pieces thrown out bit by bit along the way, whatever was left in the end burned and put unclaimed in a closet.

I never learned where our body came from or if we had her consent. After our first year, a state law was passed, placing stricter restriction on the bodies' provenance and final place of rest. Some high-profile donor had, after dissection, been buried by accident in a potter's field. He had signed up for a tidy cremation. There were, still are, mass graves on an island in the Sound, ten miles from the school, the largest mass graveyard in the country. Convicts in white jumpsuits bury bodies there for fifty cents an hour, stack pine boxes in neat rows three deep and five wide. The trenches for babies hold up to a thousand. After a century of epidemics and mundane city deaths, there are a million people buried there. You can't visit without an escort from the Department of Corrections. A carved stone by the ferry launch reads BLESSED ARE THE POOR IN SPIRIT, FOR THEIRS IS THE KINGDOM OF HEAVEN.

We would go out sometimes, the group from anatomy, though the country-house man rarely made it. He didn't drink. He may have been underage, in fact—of note, we never asked. So the Texan, and the other woman, whose name was June, and me. We were in one of those bars full of television screens, tuned to sports and nightly news broadcasts with subtitles—*crowds cheering, scattered applause*—unrelated background music loud and exhausting, when we heard on the news that a man with Ebola virus rode the subway from the hospital all the way out to an outer borough. He had done this to go to a bowling alley. The man from Texas had never heard anything so funny.

I was raised with a reverence for catastrophe. The thought of mass casualties—in the hospital, they call this Code D—has haunted me since I was a child. Back then I had a recurring dream that a trap I had crafted on the bottom bunk of my bed had filled up with the dead and dying bodies of my family, neighbors, and friends. Despite this, or perhaps because of it, I've always been a little nuts for plague literature and films, the desiccated bodies, heads hung back, mouths agape, leaning on each other in church pews, THE END IS NEAR graffitied on the walls, that sort of thing. The Texan, as much as I could hear, was describing the chaos that Ebola would bring to the city—people bleeding out on the subway, in the streets—with a speculative masculine glee.

I learned about Ebola in middle school from a video played on a rolled-in TV. Afterward I couldn't close my eyes for weeks without seeing piles of bloody bodies with flies in their eyes, Croix-Rouge in white aprons over yellow Tyvek suits, graves marked with crossed plywood, the names written in marker. I had nightmares of pine coffins the size of children, wrapped in floral paper. The outbreaks in West Africa, the video said, were made worse by the local funeral customs: washing the bodies by hand, crying over them, cooking and sleeping beside them. The remedy arranged by well-meaning foreigners was mandatory cremation, so families kept bodies hidden in their homes, and whole households were lost this way, bleeding out from everywhere.

The city emergency departments stocked up on gloves and suits and made pop-up containment tents to prepare for an outbreak that never came. Later he gave a lecture on infectious disease, the man who rode the subway with Ebola. Of course he was a doctor. He had slides. I went to the lecture, I think, to make peace with or face up to something, or just to see the flies in the eyes again, the way you sometimes can't help wanting to. But mostly he talked about medicine for HIV, cleaner water, mosquito nets. He really cared about West Africa. I still remember that night, the news, the Texan. I don't know if he couldn't tell or didn't care how much he was upsetting me. Few things for some people are only in theory.

This fascination with disaster, both fear and fetish, I never quite outgrew. The truth is, you start to sort of wish for it. Like some Czech said: Vertigo is something other than the fear of falling. Half the rush is wanting it. Wanting to get it over with.

But you wouldn't believe the parties they had, the students. The women in dresses with shoulders bare and necklines down to the navel, the men in well-cut suits. They would take the bags from inside boxes of boxed wine and drink directly from them, the bag held suspended over the drinker's head. And there were ski trips, boat trips, field trips, orchard trips for apple-picking, all of this laid out and arranged for everyone who could afford it. The well-off came to be fast friends. They had a rock band, a theater troupe, and a midsize symphony orchestra.

The body, the West Indian lady. I had a habit of holding her hand at the wrist, even after her fingers were skinned. We would tug the bared tendons to marvel at her fingers' bend, her thumb come to life like an empty crab claw after dinner at a seafood place. Those first months were a shakedown by worth, and some of us could quickly tell we were coming out toward the bottom. I, for instance, was not thriving; although for the most part I would present myself at lectures, I would return to my room at the end of the day and close the shades and stream syndicated crime dramas or simply stare at the walls. I tried not to let myself wonder too often just what I thought I was doing there. You might get the impression from this description that I easily settled into a featureless, mechanical existence—I did. It was hard to tell from the outset whether this was new or had always been latently within me. All my life, when left alone, I have often fallen listless and done literally nothing or boredly engaged in the kind of self-harm you see in captive animals. Maybe we were all like that.

There was a gym in the dorm's basement and a pressure from the cohort to become or remain remarkably fit. In a country forty percent obese, we had two fat students in a class of more than a hundred. In the gym, you'd see every stair machine, elliptical, and treadmill in use, svelte students in headphones memorizing enzymes of metabolism or the nerves of the brachial plexus on tablets propped inches from their sweat-stitched brows. It is hard to imagine the stakes of the whole lives these people had come from. That first year you'd see students leave midweek with suitcases, dejected, headed home or to an inpatient unit to recuperate. And though I believe most of them came back, they usually stayed silent on the topic of what had come over them.

There were deaths, of course, and there were vanishings. In a city of tall buildings, it was the young doctors who tended to jump off. When a resident died, announcements were made, referring the other students to the proper places to go for emotional support, and the terraces were closed for the installation of protective fencing. The missing ones were often feared to have gone over the bridge, and often they had, and would be found later after the river had pulled them back and forth. The river—it was in fact a tidal estuary—was the backdrop of the dormitory and the view from half the rooms in the hospital. In the winter as the water froze you could watch the loose ice gather and clot where the land narrowed for the footing of the bridge, and the doctors liked to point to it, the dynamics, the reversal of flow at the bottleneck, a metaphor for junky carotids. It's true you start to see the world like that. There was a long walk I'd often take from one train to another on a street with a slow traffic of people who were poor and poorly cared for, and I could count the feet sawed off from diabetes or catch the gait that meant the feet were on their way out.

The school held a memorial for the donor bodies when enough time had passed, when the students could face the families without a sense of blood on their hands. One son shared that his father was a priest of Santeria, and he placed black candles on the makeshift shrine of photographs and flowers. Which body was his, I wondered, and wondered only half as a joke which students he might have cursed for pulling him to pieces that semester. On the last day of anatomy, we changed our clothes together one last time, gathered our scrubs in trash bags, and threw away our shoes, two hundred shoes piled in a bin, like the aftermath of some atrocity.

Bedside Manner

There is something I want to tell you so we can agree that it matters. It's about my last patient, the last for now, a younger woman with a slow encephalitis, a spreading inflammation in the tissues of her brain. In an early draft I had been calling her the woman with encephalitis, because giving her a name that can't be her own felt so false. But now I am calling her Ada, and the false name is starting to fill up with her and hurt in another way. I miss her.

She had been fine, just fighting fevers once we had the seizures under control. But then she began to forget things, like the year or her address or the last thing she ate or the last thing she said. Despite all of our tests, we did not know why she was still losing her mind. After a while she was in a coma, and I would sit with her husband after a long day, wishing I were home. He told me how they met. There was only one chair in the room by her bed, so I sat on a step stool near his feet like a child. While he spoke, he laughed a lot and looked at his wife as though he could see through her into the past. All manner of things, I thought, can be well.

While she was awake, Ada had a view of the river and kept a set of binoculars by the window. In my downtime I would sit in a chair and examine the opposite shore. I knew from my walks outside the hospital that men fished on the banks along that river, and on the streets between delis and dollar stores, Dominicans played checkers on legless tables the players balanced on their knees. An old arsenal beside the hospital housed the largest men's shelter in the city. During the day, shelter men would stagger the streets high on synthetic marijuana—just oregano or some other plant matter sprayed with chemicals made in a lab, labeled SPICE or SMOKING INCENSE and sold behind the counter in the delis. The men who smoked it had red-stained fingers and would freeze in place, dazed, and sometimes even stand stock-still in the street, as if they were dreaming. This was the neighborhood, but not what you saw from Ada's window. Her view was a bland line of condos and trees shrouding paths along the opposite side of the river.

We were only killing time. Because her arms were black with bruises, and she couldn't remember what any of the tests were for no matter how often we reminded her, she would shout and swear at the staff. When her husband couldn't be there to redirect her, she would often end up tied to the bed for trying to get up or taking a swing at someone. And then, just as fast, like an amnesiac on television, she would come back to us, blinking, and ask, Where am I?

I don't know what it means to suffer. I try to feel it out. When someone is dying and then they die, what hits you first is relief, permissiveness, a broad calm for a moment: world without end. Then some deaths just grab you by the throat, remind you of the balance of the game. Remember looking in the mirror as a child, saying your name? This face, you'd think, these hands. This house and yard and mother, going to bed without dinner on cabbage night, jumping from the roof of the shed. The bravery of it all, the obvious import. But this is how it ends: surrounded by strangers, your clothes cut off with shears, cold blue hands, and gone then, with your body humiliated and left alone to stiffen. In the trauma bay once I watched this, a cardiac arrest, the patient gone too long for us to be able to bring him back. A nurse got a shock from an ill-timed defibrillator and fell to the floor, unattended. I picked up his wallet—not the nurse's, the dead man's—which was worn from the specific ways he had handled it but was now done forever with being in his hands. When my great loss comes, I hope I scream like his wife and fall to the floor, not keep still and silent as my heart explodes in my chest.

The obvious, a poet said, is difficult to prove. The hard part is I want to tell the truth. Meaning what, exactly? We are schooled in taking, not giving, a history. We are taught to reach first for open-ended questions. How you ask can earn an answer closer to the truth. For example, you don't ask someone if she drinks; you say, How much do you drink on the average day? You don't ask if someone is compliant with his medication; you ask, How often do you miss a dose? We are told to normalize our queries about drugs, sex, and death by asking them to everyone. But in practice you will not ask a healthy young person or a child's parents if they want to be resuscitated when their heart stops, and you will not ask a frail old grandmother if she has sex with men, women, or both. And we run tests, anyway, for the real truth. Try to lie on a serum test for syphilis. People will certainly surprise you.

We had a man once who smoked cocaine in his hospital bed while admitted for active tuberculosis. The doctors laughed about this, laughed at him, behind doors, in other rooms. What are we even doing here, they said, laughing, to one another—meaning this was not someone who was going to get well. On the other hand, who would?

Some morbid social scientists ran studies in a lab where volunteers took a test on an unrelated subject while the screen flashed small subliminal messages, pictures of skulls or graves, I guess, or words like *death,* some classic unsubtle memento mori. Afterward, in a variety of surveys, the subjects who were primed with death reminders showed some dark and predictable tendencies. They were racist, for example, and would behave with overt hostility toward people who appeared to be from different cultural or religious groups. The scientists let the subjects force the out-group strangers to take shots of sriracha, a validated measure of aggression known as hot-sauce allocation. They supposed that the provoked bigotry was the subjects' way of making meaning, of asserting their belonging to a group that would be here after they die. The social scientists dubbed this terror management—our dull means of evading death's aggressive senselessness.

I brought it up at a dinner party once. I had been invited out with two classmates by a dean to a club in town, a club for members only. The rooms had tall drapes on tall windows, leather chairs hunched around fireplaces, obscene martinis each served with a second metal glass. The dean, of course, was a doctor too, and occasionally wrote poetry. He had selected us personally for a discussion of the arts. I thought a poet-doctor should be as game as anyone for talking about death, but he wouldn't even let me get started. The classmates, both men and poets too, talked the way we were meant to, about schools they had attended, traveling abroad, minor celebrities they all knew in common. On the tour of the club we took after cocktails, there was a painting, smaller than a breadbox, kept behind a little curtain to protect it from the light. Although the curtain was pulled back for us, I don't recall the painting in the slightest.

I'd wanted to ask the dean how our terror might be managed in the hospital, where we walk around primed with death all day and care—it has been shown—more poorly for the poor and the disabled and people of color, groups from which doctors largely do not come. The dean and the poets and I all were white; in fact, everyone at the club that I could see was white except the man who served the enormous martinis. The dinner was one with courses and all kinds of forks and different wines to match the different meats. I had a drunk, underwater feeling by the time it was time to leave. I managed, I think, not to say much of anything.

The taxi drivers were on strike that week, so I walked fifty blocks home with one of the poets. He said he planned to become a brain surgeon. He was from an Orthodox Jewish family, but he wanted me to know he didn't believe in all that and that he objected to anything he couldn't prove. All sandpiles have the same slope, I told him, and no one knows why. Is that true? he asked. It might be. If not, there is still gravity, there is still time, still the way it sometimes seems to matter that any of us were even born. He said he had nearly died just before he was a teenager—leukemia— and while his family took his survival as a sign from above, he finished chemotherapy as an atheist. He wanted to know what I believed. These were the conversations I always started after being out drinking, though I never wanted to answer the kinds of questions I asked. He said he hated hobbies, hated leisure, hated music—any diversion without immediate use. His indulgences were cooking and the artful plating of food. And poetry, of course. I later learned that his was terrible, all literal and grim. He did have one about a barbecue that ended in a way I sort of liked: Some days it is hard to believe / everyone dies only once.

And just try to be a smoker in a place like this. When my classmates found me with a cigarette on the corners where I hid between lectures, they would avert their eyes or actually cross the street in silence. But a few of them—even June and the Texan, always after they had been drinking, with or without me—often sought me out and asked for one for a treat. Once I was on the corner with just the Texan, and one of the shelter men approached us. He must have missed last call, gotten locked out for the night. His speech was slurred but I gathered he was after a cigarette. He stood too near to us, swaying a little. I worked the lighter for him and he thanked me and left. And the Texan said, That was a close one. He helped lead a clinic where the students practiced taking histories and doing physicals on the homeless. He said he could stand the shelter men in the clinic, but on the street they made him sick. Is that wrong? he wanted to know, but why would I be the one to tell him?

The clinic was in a church basement in a Blacker part of town. It, too, was a club for members only. In our year, it was run by the Texan and a woman on a military scholarship—one way to afford the six-figure tuition. She did not have the teeth of a person raised poor, but why else would you join the military? I had applied for a spot at the clinic too. You had to write an essay. I did not know yet that you aren't allowed to talk about poverty from the inside. You could only look back on it. I wrote about never having health insurance, knowing how it feels to be sick and afraid. But the clinic decided, the Texan said, to go in a different direction.

I voted for you, he said in earnest. But he had to let me know I'd provoked some ill will among my classmates, particularly the woman in the military. She was upset, he said, over something I had said in psychiatry class. They let you practice on them as well, the patients with psychiatric illness; they consent because they don't know not to. They had brought in a small, middle-aged Ecuadoran man who stood before the class and answered questions about why he had been locked up. He was wearing pajama pants and a hospital gown with another gown over it backwards, like a cape. He had been escorted through the open air from the hospital to the lecture hall by a pair of student volunteers. His condition, his disorder, was that he tended to believe you were in love with him. *You* being anyone. And he lost his job after making passes at his boss, left his wife, and now had been tossed from his uncle's house, for he had thought even that grizzled old man was in love with him. And he had an enamored and heartsick way of telling all this, because at first when he was locked up, he knew his doctor was in love with him, but now on the pills they made him take, he had a shake in his hands and no idea who loved him. The doctor leading the class, a man with slick hair and a keen interest in what's called bench research, asked the man if he could have been mistaken about the boss, the uncle, the doctor upstairs. No, he said. They all did love me once.

So much of medicine is just learning the words for things. In psychiatry, for example, hallucination is perception without an object, while illusion is true perception interpreted incorrectly, like seeing tree branches as reaching arms or hearing murmured voices in the susurrus of running water. A delusion is a deeply held belief that is either false or at least—said the doctor leading the class—unshared by your community. This struck me as an odd caveat. I imagined any truth-teller, Copernicus or whoever, meeting the criteria for delusional disorder. Is the exception, I asked him in class, for religion? Is the delusion of chosen ones, of resurrection, of the reign of an all-knowing sky man somehow less insane if enough of us agree to share it? You don't have to say things like that, the Texan told me later. The woman in the military was evangelical and offended. I have seen her in pictures, beaming in fatigues, posing with guns of all shapes and sizes, even the large lead-pipe ones that shoot rockets or grenades.

In a special section on brain pathology, I watched a fetus have an autopsy. The limp little body was draped over a chunk of two-by-four. The mother had contracted Zika, the latest virus, the one that makes fetal brains stay small and smooth and useless. And so they'd pulled him out, pulled it out, the fetus, therapeutically. The skull was split like an old tomato, and the little limbs lay limp, almost translucent, the perfect hands and fingers of someone who would never use them. The doctors who cut him up spoke over him about, I remember, the weather, a new pair of shoes, a rumor regarding a new pavilion. But can you imagine killing anyone you didn't have to?

In case you ever wondered, when they take out your organs during an autopsy, they store them all together in a large plastic bag labeled with your name and hospital identification number. Your brain is fixed in fixative and placed in a Rubbermaid box like one might store extra pencils in. I asked where the parts go off to then, but the people I asked didn't know.

I pray only in dreams where I am dying, and I often die in my dreams, or am dying, buried in rubble after an explosion or in a falling elevator or a crashing plane. But in waking life, I'll still sometimes get an urge to pray, on the subway, say, in the tunnel parts that wind under rivers, or on the bridges, or when there is smoke in a station, or when the lights go out on the train, or when some man on the train starts yelling, yelling at me, looking in my eyes until I look away: Fucking cunt, fucking bitch, I'm about to blow your head off. Just as an example. There is one prayer I know will be answered: *Lord, let me suffer a lot and then let me die.* But I know also Our Father and some psalms; I know faith is the substance of things hoped for and that the evil of the day is sufficient thereof. And I am jealous, sometimes, of the lives of my peers or patients or families who find comfort in icons or in saying the rosary, who keep from collapsing in the face of tragedy by leaving some book with heavy pages open significantly on the bed. It's too easy to dismiss the comforts you cannot have.

After the dinner at the club, the very next day, I got called to the office of that dean. Because I was afraid or for whatever reason, I put it off for weeks. When I did go, I found he did not want to see me but had left for me a copy of a poem written by a woman who had been born and also buried in the city where I was born. It said, among other things: The doctors should fear arrogance more than cardiac arrest. I didn't know, and didn't ask, if this meant him or me.

Clinical Reasoning

They set us loose in the preoperative waiting room, where patients sat before being rolled off into surgery. It was still on the dark side of dawn, and I was assigned to cardiothoracic service. That first day, before I knew better, I asked a man awaiting valve surgery if he was afraid. He was with his wife and his father, and it was the ruddy old father who took the most offense. What the hell kind of question is that? he asked. As though we were sitting in an airplane waiting to take off. *Nervous* was okay to say, everyone was nervous, but no one was allowed to be afraid.

The man was young and they were replacing one of the valves in his heart. Interns came around with markers to mark the spot where each patient would be cut open, and then the attending surgeons came by separately to initial the spots to confirm. Cutting on the wrong side or cutting out the wrong part was common enough to warrant permanent markers. The valve patient was confused when they came to him and marked a spot on the side of his ribs. He had thought they planned to crack him open at the sternum. It's a new technique, the intern said. Noninvasive. The man seemed disappointed. They are giving him a valve from a horse's heart, his father said. After this, he will be part horse. The father winked at me, and the wife looked at the floor. It was actually a porcine valve, meaning it came from a pig.

I grew up in a ruined generation. The problem, they said, was that everyone got a prize. It was also a time of running lockdown drills in schools for when some loner came to kill us. They had just stopped teaching the useless practice of hiding under desks from atom bombs, but they would line us up in the halls in child's poses for the tornado-warning sirens. The shooter drills started just after Columbine—code red. The teacher would lock the door and then we'd wait in silence. Gunshots, we were taught, would be a rhythmic popping without production of smoke. This was called code silver in the hospital, and we did not have to practice for it. But out of habit, in lecture halls, I still planned paths to escape and developed fearful fascinations with my quieter classmates—one in particular, always with a wide stance and sobbing in the stalls of the mixed-gender bathroom. It's just as likely he was afraid of me.

A television commercial for a cancer center said: Less fear. More science.

I spent a lot of time with Ada's husband once she was in her coma. I wish I could remember every word of what he told me. He had a white-hot purity of heart you never see in real life, like something from a work of art.

A study showed that if you are bleeding into your head in an American hospital, the factor that affects prognosis most is whether or not you speak English. A doctor told me this, a man in charge, and followed it by sighing. English was his second or third language, but he could not get his residents to use interpreters, even the ones you just call on the phone. The phone had Spanish, Mandarin, Haitian Creole, even Belarusian— but the trainee doctors didn't have time for that. In the ward where Ada lay in her coma, the residents replaced speech with pressure applied to the base of the thumbnail with the side of a pen or penlight. They would write in their notes under mental status: Withdraws to noxious stimuli x4. When the thumbnail cracked, they would switch to the index finger, and so on through the hand.

Doctors, it seems, really do think language is secondary, that nothing spoken can amount to more than the vital signs, the labs, the imaging. But I couldn't help wondering if they refused to use interpreters because they didn't want to be heard, or to be witnessed, faltering through the procedure of speech. There is a strange intimacy to having your words, however hastily chosen, processed through a whole other person. Maybe it is an issue of trust.

A young woman had been in a motorcycle accident. A tough part of the hospital narrative, aside from the fear of liability, is that every room is the same, and in every room, in every bed, a body in the same outfit. In the genre of hospital narrative, I have noticed a tendency to artfully describe the tone of skin, the shape of eyes. At least one nose must be aquiline. This was a Black woman with a swollen brain from a motorcycle accident, and if you'd seen her, you would have had a hard time even thinking what her nose was shaped like, because you would be more interested in the rest of her head—half her skull had been sawed off so her brain had room to expand, and there were patches elsewhere where her hair had been shaved and holes drilled for probes that measured the damage. Holes and metal rods and wires everywhere. They called this apparatus the *bundle,* cute as it was not. They, the doctors, took to scrawling meticulous notes by hand on a grid of squares with a space for every hour—what were the salts, the chemicals, the pressures. Am I allowed to say this was an experiment? And around her, a whole family hoping for the best.

We don't have a class on the history of malpractice or on the role of physicians in war crimes or genocides. But on the wards, we did learn quickly that Black families, more than most, did not trust the doctors. When a Black patient was dying on life support, the attendings would often say not to bother telling the family that there wasn't any hope. Those kinds of families, we were told, never pull the plug.

The flyers recruiting for the Tuskegee experiment read, *You may feel well and still have bad blood! Come and bring your families.* Hundreds of Black men enrolled. Those who were found to have syphilis weren't told or treated. They were fed a hot meal at each checkup, and after they died and were autopsied, their families were given fifty dollars with which to bury them. That penicillin cures syphilis was discovered ten years into the study, but it was not given to the men of Tuskegee, whose diseased cadavers were the study's aim and prize. The experiment was halted by public outrage forty years after it started, when the story was leaked to the *New York Times*. The last physician in charge of the experiment, the head, at the time, of the Centers for Disease Control, stressed that patients weren't denied lifesaving drugs, they just weren't offered any. The Tuskegee experiment ended the same year Bob Barker started hosting *The Price Is Right*.

You don't even need to say *Tuskegee* to explain it, the Texan said. I mean, look around. What people of color face in regular life is worse in the hospital by an order of magnitude—ten thousand little violences every day.

In that ward, the neuroscience intensive care unit, there was bed after bed of silent women and men in a blanket noise of ventilators and cheerful alarm tones:

help-me, help-me, I-cannot-breathe. And you'd get a sense that the doctors felt embarrassed to talk to them, even though we all knew that no one could say what they might be awake to. I was required to pinch them, for my notes and presentations on rounds. I learned to say I'm sorry: Désolée, lo siento.

The woman in the bundle was shipped off eventually to long-term acute care. It is hard to know who will recover and how much from that kind of brain injury. Among themselves, her doctors gave a laughing prognosis: She'll never play chess again.

Reaction Formation

This was in the emergency ward for psych patients. The doors stayed locked and the guards were armed. The patient was a young woman with fresh cuts up both her arms, ticks like marking time. The thin white doctor didn't ask her why. The psychiatrists will tell you that it is never a good move to take a trauma history. The patients love to rehash it, they just go on and on. But how could it not matter if she had been abused as a child, beaten by her mother, or neglected, or if some stepfather had asked her for a favor, asked her to go to the basement to change the washed clothes over to the dryer, say, and watched her down the dark wet steps, then closed the door and locked it? Maybe she was afraid after that, of men or of the dark. Maybe she always had been.

Doctors call these patients borderline. Depression is a mood disorder, something wrong with how you feel. Borderline is a personality disorder, something wrong with who you are.

Her hair had been done. Blown out, you could see, with a round brush. Like all of the patients in the ward, she'd been removed from her clothes and put in a gown, and her shoes had been taken and she'd been given socks with rubber treads on the bottoms and on the tops so that there was no way they could be put on upside down. The doctor spoke very softly, steepling his fingers below his chin. This seemed meant to make him appear gentle, approachable, but just served to make the woman have to lean in close to hear him. Over his soft voice, you could hear shouting from the hall, even with the door closed, and see through the glass the voice's source: a strong young man with tattooed arms shouting over and over: *That's not a promise, it's a threat.*

The doctor had been looking for disorganized thought. He asked her if she ever felt that things in the world had a special significance. Like what? The radio, the newscast, the shape of the clouds. She said she'd been counting streetlights. That whenever she walked under them, they went out.

A new building had sprung up across the river. It was all made of glass with a tint that made it disappear in certain conditions of light. You could see only the ribs, the window frames. It looked about a hundred stories high. Who would even want to live there, so up in the air like that? asked a woman whose father was dying in the ICU. We were at his bedside. The hope was to send him home on hospice, but he had made the mistake of coming to terms with his imminent death in the late afternoon on a Friday, so he was stuck with us at least through the weekend. I bet the floors sway in the wind up there, she said. I bet it stirs the ice in your glass. And I agreed. I said: I don't think I could live like that.

An example of classical conditioning. They took a baby, nine months old, a stolid and unemotional infant, per report, and exposed him to a white rat over and over while striking a steel bar with a hammer behind his head. Little Albert. He quickly learned to scream at just the sight of the rat and then extrapolated further, screaming at dogs, furs, bearded Santas. His mother, prudent at the worst possible moment, pulled him from the study before the process could be reversed. She had been paid one dollar for his time.

We still do a lot of harm to rats, at least. In an animal model for post-traumatic stress, rats were locked in colored cages and administered electric shocks, then moved to other-colored cages and observed to see how they reacted. Certain rats did not relax, couldn't tell the difference, kept waiting for the current to come light them up. These were the pathological rats. Researchers examined these troubled rats' genetics, looking for the exomes that coded for their poor resilience. Elsewhere, in concussion studies, they built a small machine, a blunt sort of rat guillotine, to give all the subjects identical head injuries.

Little Albert, of course, is not a sad story about a rat.

They had to hold her in the emergency ward for seventy-two hours, the mandatory sentence for considering suicide. She had a boyfriend or some kind of partner who waited outside for the brief time visitors were allowed, the most beautiful man any of us had probably ever seen. He kept trying to break her out. He would chase the thin white doctor through the halls outside the ward. The patient was white;

the partner too. Otherwise it is hard to imagine the doctors would have put up with them. It's true there was nothing to do for her, so they kept her quiet on antipsychotics and in bed. As a compromise, the guards let the boyfriend bring coffee in as long as it was cold. The cot beside hers held a woman who spoke no English and sobbed at all hours, drowning out the Spanish-language television.

It was a mistake, the boyfriend said. The thin sharp marks all down her arms, the same size as little staples. Bringing her here, he said. Sometimes she would cry and he would sit beside her on the bed, and the armed guard would shout: Don't do that.

The treatment she needed, dialectical behavioral therapy, took many weeks and used worksheets. The psychologist who invented this intervention called these patients the most miserable people in the world.

Upstairs there were whole wards full of people who'd gone mad, gone off their medication, started stripping in the streets. They cried at night for born and unborn children. The doctors thought up new sets of pills as they sat around a table every morning. They often repeated that electroshock therapy had gotten a bad rap. I would go into the treatment room with a man who had lost his children to time and neglect and who worried, without end, about a shed full of car parts he needed to get rid of. You are like a daughter to me, he said the day we met. When I'd walk him into the little room—just a gurney and a setup for some light anesthesia—he'd say he was afraid.

Maybe after that stepfather left and before the next one came, she would go down on her own and climb into the dryer, full of towels still warm. The Buddhists will tell you not to get attached to what is, after all, only a pleasant sensation.

An older student rotating through the ward was planning to become a psychiatrist. He had oiled hair and a bad turn to his lips that made him look like a villain from television. He said it was a common misconception that you had to value soft skills to want to work in mental health. Look at us, this locked unit, he said. The patients will give you anything. They need to be led. Can you imagine another way to own a person so entirely? He had gone to Vienna or wherever just to lie on Freud's couch.

It's true you can't help feeling that they might be to blame. The depressives especially don't even seem to try. The drugs these people take make them fat and flat of affect. Everyone's hands shake all the time. When they do the shock treatments, they paralyze the patient, so only the mind has a seizure. Can you hold my hand? the sad man asked, but that didn't seem appropriate. He was vacant afterward, when they rolled him out, with blood on his mouth from where he had bitten his lip. How did I get so old? he would sometimes lament. I take so many vitamins.

The borderlines make for easy questions on the exams we have to take. Always a woman poised to kill herself: superficial threats, superficial cuts. Wanting attention, or what else? Somehow all these women have been raped or assaulted in some way, and what they lose is the internal conviction that they are a person in any real sense. Identity disintegrates. But human character, it has been said, is just a vital lie. I can see the woman with the cut-up arms walk out with her beautiful boyfriend through a glass house, an atrium that used to be the space between two buildings. A nurse on the way out had said to her: Don't ever come back here again. Her head on his shoulder. Before they're out of sight, she lights a cigarette.

Medical students show up on the exams sometimes too, but even there we are overaccomplished. The answer to the medical-student question will always be sleep deprivation, OCD, or the overuse of prescription stimulants.

I did ask Ada once if she was afraid. Ada with her binoculars, her soft encephalitis. She didn't have the words anymore to answer. There was a boat I had noticed from my room at night. Even our little dorms, our cold rooms with old linoleum floors, faced the estuary. A small boat, no name or signage, always going to the same spot and stopping in the night. Now, through the binoculars, I got no hints. Drug run? Treasure hunt? I'd seen on that river a Jet Ski sink just at the foot of the bridge. And I walked across the bridge and back, just once, and was struck by the shaking of the traffic. A guard there told me about the jumpers. He said the worst were the ones who missed the river and hit the rocks or the concrete blocks below. The guard had a desperate and apologetic tone from having to keep saying things nobody wanted to hear.

One more from the psych ward. A woman whose husband had died of a heart attack. They had come in together, the man dead, the wife ready. She told me rather calmly that she had never had much appetite for life outside of her husband. She said: Keep me a day, and when I leave I will kill myself. Keep me a month, and when I leave I will kill myself. And so on. She was hard to blame. There are countries where you can get yourself euthanized for depression, chronic illness, disability—or just the firm feeling that your life is now complete. What more could we hope for? I sometimes feel this way myself, or wonder which versions of life are worth living.

In the class where they teach us the physical exam, we practice on each other. In this way I have been diagnosed with crooked spine, water on the knee, paroxysmal vertigo, and sensorineural hearing loss. I am in awe of the students who touch me. They are always so clean, as though they were taught how to bathe, how to do laundry, in ways I was not, as though they spend hours every day cleaning beneath their fingernails. But we did all get carsick when they sent us by taxi to a community hospital to learn from a family practice doctor who baked for us each week. We would be green from the traffic and ungrateful for these gifts, all breads made with zucchini or unripe tomatoes.

Believe me, a playwright said, there are people out

there who do not love you. One of my classmates got a whim to go learn Portuguese. She said we should all take less and do more, and she borrowed money from her parents for tickets to Brazil. I let myself down and spent that first summer in some collegiate suburb, living with a seminarian, earning beer money by writing copy for press releases and grants, the best of which concerned powering cars with a particle theory of gravity.

Another thing I did that summer for money was participate in research studies. I was not selected as a normal control in a study of functional MRI mapping, but they did let me enroll in a trial about cigarette smoking. They had me smoke through a foot-long tube stuck through a hole in the spine of a plastic binder, to blind me, I think, to the cigarette? And sometimes the tube had special filters in it, and sometimes the cigarette was a placebo—dried lettuce, the research assistant said. All this happened in a hospital room, if you can imagine, with a desk in the place where the bed would be. The pay was three hundred dollars.

The seminarian was writing a thesis on the very early Christians, the ones who kicked around getting martyred while Paul or whoever wrote the New Testament. They were mostly, he told me, pacifist, egalitarian, and queer. And they were obsessed with the body, fascinated with the incarnation, that there was something so crucial about existing as a body that even God had to try it out. They didn't even have a story of what Jesus died for yet. It was just a mysterious thing that had happened. He said these early Christians stood still and silent on the floor of the Colosseum as gladiators stabbed them or lions tore them to pieces, depressing the crowds, who had come to see a spectacle. They believed in universal salvation, he told me, and a real resurrection of the body for everyone. Later theologians tried to pull this back to mind-body dualism by debating the shape these resurrected bodies would take. One professor asserted that the resurrected body should possess the most perfect shape—the sphere—in homage to the divine and spherical shape of the human head.

Remember the bundle? I don't know what happened to that woman after she left. The brain has a number of reflexes to lose before you're dead. And she—she just kept them. On rounds every day we would say her name, and the nurse would comment:

A very strong cough. To everyone there, she was just taking up a bed. But a new man across the way, he was bundle material. Despite his age, which the doctors, by bias, called a healthy eighty-six, his sudden bleed and wild swelling would make a good case for the spreadsheets. The family, sadly, said no way. And the fellow asked if we should talk to them about withdrawal—that is, taking the tubes out and letting him get on his way. No, the attending said. He's had an operation. We'll need to survive him at least thirty days. The surgeons really were God's gift, they said. A rumor was they all ate less than a thousand calories a day, since a mouse model showed this was the best way to live forever. And they got graded on the percentage of their patients that lived a month, which was not too hard to pull off if you had the right equipment.

I love a lot of things I have lost. It barely bothers me now. I can pull my heart out over work and then go home to nothing. I sleep like the dead. There are things, of course, that could be better. I was shadowing the hospice doctors on a case, a very old man, thirty-one days post-op, who would not wake up. He wasn't in a coma but had what we call delirium: a syndrome of waxing and waning wake-fulness, agitation, and hallucinations common in the elderly when they are hospitalized. Survivors call it a waking nightmare with themes of restraint, captivity, and sexual assault, a reasonable way to interpret being tied to a bed and penetrated with needles and catheters. Because he was as confused as Ada was, he too was strapped down with padded shackles to keep him from tearing out the IVs or the breathing tube. His attention mostly waned, but sometimes he would track me with his eyes, and once he wrote a note in large crude script that said only: Kill me. I had asked what he hoped would happen next.

The hospice doctor spoke with a slow, calm willingness that made you believe there were worse things than death. He was short and divorced and a well-traveled Buddhist. I don't know what he thought of me. But for our patient, he tried his best. One treatment for prolonged and likely terminal delirium is called palliative sedation. We tried it for one day, and the drugs calmed the man enough that they could take the straps off his wrists. He had purple bangles of deep bruises around each of them. But the surgeons wanted to cut again, place a tube in his throat for breathing and another in his belly to feed him. They told his son the hospice doctors hadn't given his father enough of a chance. You can't win them all, the hospice doctor told me in the hallway. They woke the man up and tied him down, and he died like that before the surgery.

The first time I watched someone die, I went to dinner afterward with a friend, a philosophy student who had never worked a day in her life. Or she had, of course, in academics and sometimes had a brief employ as a barback or a clerk in a dessert shop, each role a kind of ruse or joke, the visors and polyblend polos some sort of poor-kid disguise. The restaurant had a long rounded ceiling with thin planks running lengthwise like the hull of an upturned boat. Over our drinks I kept turning it over, perseverating: Where are we all going, where did the dead man go? She was bored of it from the start. Why, she said, does this have you so stuck? It was always the friends who put the whole meal on their fathers' credit cards who liked to say I ate too fast. Let's try, she said, to enjoy it. What I ordered came, to my surprise, with its head still on.

Months later, when we went out some tired night

while I was in school and counting out a long string of eighty-hour weeks, she said that, really, some of us were not meant for work. Meaning her, I guess. She said, Why do you think everybody needs to have a job?

The school brought in a famous philanthropist to tell us how to do the most good in the world. His organization had done a cost-benefit analysis, and using the data, he argued that we should focus on those the worst off to start—hang nets for malaria, treat cholera, dig wells. His study results implied we had enough high-end medicine already. What this whole subject had to do with a roomful of young elites planning careers in orthopedic surgery, luxury cars picked out in advance, was unclear. More than one of my classmates had proudly explained to me how much income they had already lost compared to friends working in finance or consulting. We were all so smart, they reminded us, or we wouldn't be here. It was rare, outside of personal statements, to find many students who believed this work was a calling. But there were still mission trips to go on during free summers or months assigned as elective time. In certain foreign countries, you could deliver babies or perform appendectomies despite a lack of any degree or skills or official training. And you could tell yourself it was better for those patients than nothing, then go off on the weekend to the nearest beach.

The seminarian says that when the world is sick, no one can be well. I believe it, but I could never sell it to my classmates. As a group, they really weren't likable at all, but every time I got one alone, even one I really couldn't stand from a distance, she would start telling me some sad story about how close she had come to being a professional tennis player or a professional figure skater until puberty hit and her body went all wrong, she stayed too short, got too fat, breasts came in too large. She was tan, with broad shoulders and too much brass in her dyed blond hair. She was, or seemed to be, from Florida—it is hard to imagine the wealthy even there. Why would you live in Florida if you could live anywhere? I had to have them reduced, she said, but it was too late already. That kind of thing always wins me over, and they were all that way one on one, though they would throw you straight under a train if it would get them honors on a clinical rotation.

The woman from the psychiatric emergency had been uninsured. The best they could do was enroll her in a research study. The undergraduate volunteer phlebotomists who worked the intake laughed at the marks on her arms and at a bruise she had on her shoulder in the shape of a set of teeth. So she never got that treatment they would have tried, a Buddhist type of behavioral therapy where you yell into pillows, clutch ice cubes to calm your rage. They were collecting a series of functional MRIs to show that domestic trauma rewired the brain the same as in combat veterans who came back shell-shocked, unable to tell the difference between threatening and unthreatening scenes. But after that one-session introduction, she did not come back. Who could blame her? I would do the very same thing.

Child Life

The nurses lined up to meet a famous baseball player. The children's hospital always pulled out all the stops. I met a girl there with epilepsy, but half her seizures were psychogenic. In the hospital, she had food to eat, cable TV, and a rotating cast of people like me to ask her how she was feeling. And I felt for her. I had also been a child who did not want to go home. There were stars paved into the floors in the halls, rocket ships painted on the MRI machine, as if we could protect the children from the rest of their lives. On the night shift I did breathing rounds, counted the rising chests of the babies with respiratory infections. A full minute each by penlight.

I met a preschool kid with sickle cell who was working through the semantic differences between similar words. He had been told that he could not go to the game room. He meant, I gathered, that he didn't care, but what he kept insisting was *I don't matter!*

At school as a kid, I learned to write by copying the Bible. For punishment, I copied it in chalk onto the board. We pledged allegiance to the Bible every morning, our hands on our hearts, and to the flag and then to the Christian flag, and memorized long passages of verses for awards. It must have been good for our vocabularies. The school did not teach science or any world history, so when it was shut down—the pastor was caught stealing and suspected of worse— and I fell into the secular school, I was in junior high and behind in a lot of things. Science did not interest me. History was familiar, at least, the war stories not unbiblical, old and new atrocities and carnage a part of the necessary landscape. But I had never heard of the Holocaust before they rolled in a TV to show videos of the liberation of Auschwitz, the sunken cheeks, the bones for arms with numbers tattooed on them. One part told of how the well-meaning soldiers had given the prisoners chocolate and other rations, and the prisoners had been starved so long that eating this actually killed them. In a seat in the dark, I sobbed and sobbed until the teacher pulled me out of class.

And said what, exactly? You see, I didn't know there were so many brands of apocalypse. We saw a video of the Mayans with their doomsday calendar and learned about, like I said, Ebola in Africa, the Spanish flu, bird flu, pig flu, the San Andreas Fault, Waco, AIDS, nuclear winter and waste and war. And then Columbine, the boys in long black coats, who we heard pointed their guns in students' faces and asked, Do you believe in God? We had practiced martyr scenarios at my old school, but now I just thought, No, no, no. I became distracted and was sent to the counselor, a social work student who covered every school in the county. She asked me this: Any trouble at home?

In my childhood home, an ongoing fight concerned the location of all the household knives. Someone would always be stealing them for carving projects in the yard or slug dissections in the basement. Scissors were even harder to find. The bathroom door lost its knob, and the scissors were the only thing that fit. You had to choose between no privacy or a room you would never get out of unless a brother came to let you out. Our poor mother, outnumbered six to one.

She drank hard twice a year and, before she got sick, would give you anything you wanted.

In the children's hospital, in the waiting room, a book meant for children asks, Why is the sky blue? And the answer begins: First, understand that colors do not really exist. On a wall nearby hangs a case of objects removed from the noses and ears of actual children, each neatly labeled:

Bean
Beetle
Fruit pit
Marble
Match
Moth
Pen part
Pin
Seed
Spring
Tack
Toothpick

My favorite operation by far was the cesarean. The woman would sit up on the gurney and get a shot that numbed her from the waist down. My job was to pull her toward me, and she would lean forward onto me, and I'd ask her small questions to distract from the large needle headed into her spine. Is this your first, I would ask, or if I got the sense the baby wasn't joyfully expected, I'd ask about her interests, her job, or her tattoos. Once she was numb, we laid her down and built a paper wall between her and where she would be cut open. The partner, if there was one, came in a space suit and stood with the anesthetist.

I saw a delivery with twins where we couldn't get a good grip on the infants. I was scrubbed in, calmed by the excitement, holding a bent spatula that kept open the hole we had made, the edges of which were red and bleeding. The first head appeared, wet and scarcely haired, but the surgeon couldn't get a good grip. Push from below, someone shouted, and someone did, going under the sterile blue paper and doing what, I can't imagine. The twins, extracted, quiet and blue, disappeared in separate rolling boxes. And I did not follow up, because there was another day coming, and I was tired.

I thought of obstetrics more than anything else, or anything else besides the job I eventually picked.

This love surprised me—I had always sort of feared women's bodies—but in the clinic, I saw young women try to defer exams when they hadn't found time to shave, and so many, especially the youngest, basically children, knew nothing about their own anatomy and even when pregnant were mortified to talk about discharge or blood. And I did like to be with them, to talk to them, to help take the shame off of bodies and sex.

I was, in a way, a bad obstetrician. As I watched the doctor free those twin blue heads, I thought it wouldn't be the worst thing if the babies were dead. The seminarian was upset when I said this. He had been coming down from the green suburban hill of his school on the weekends. We would drink wine from chalices he had bought in Rome. There wasn't much that we agreed on. We did both believe my heart was kind, and I could not explain my feeling about the babies. I just kept saying: I mean, they haven't even done anything yet.

The summer I lived with him, writing copy, we slept side by side in a twin bed and never had sex. Our relationship existed but could not be called anything. It felt like a third body in the room with us on those weekend visits. I would go on about cell biology or the odd and arrogant rituals of my classmates. He would suggest only by expressions of his face that I lacked generosity or was too quick to judge. He sometimes reminded me that I, too, would be rich when all of this was over. But I had not yet shown him the receipts, all the loans I'd had to take, all I owed for this and what I had done before it.

You're acting out a childhood fantasy, the Texan said. We were becoming friends, inasmuch as he gave me little doses of the drugs he ordered from local teenagers by text message and sometimes, without context, late at night, would send me links to gay pornography with brief notes like: My favorite. It was always slick young men just bending each other over. I had confessed to him—the Texan—that I did not believe in anything and that this departure from religion, obvious and unvolitional, was the probable cause of my recurrent dreams of praying as I died in freak accidents. He found my celibate union with a theology student odd and repressive but could not help admitting that the seminarian was unusually attractive. A real magazine man, was what he called him. The Texan's sexual orientation, as far as I could tell, was anyone who would have him. But the point of finding God is not that you want to have sex with him.

It's not true, anyway, to say I don't believe in *any-thing*. I believe in a blind eye / in a deaf ear / in a lame foot. I don't believe in this world empty. All of this, of course, is stolen poetry.

The seminarian told me that, in the seventies, a group of divinity students were given LSD and put in a church basement where they listened to a Good Friday sermon alongside a control group dosed with a placebo. One of the men (they were all men) remembered a sense of being absorbed in bars of light, then the physical pain of having all his insides ripped out, then dying and being resurrected. He recalled, at that very moment, the preacher through the speakers said: I shall die, but that is all I'll do for death.

Almost all of the drugged seminarians went on to become ministers, and not one in the control group did. What's the point? I asked, sincerely, and we debated what mattered more, the reason for the experience or the experience itself. Some months later, when I took the train up the hill and in his little room we shared a single small mushroom, we did not see God, but we did both see, all at once, that in a portrait on the wall that he had gotten at a junk shop, the brushstrokes built up a shape like a skull beneath the man's face—an incidental memento mori. And after that we did all the things two people who don't have sex can do.

The psychiatry attending sent me out for a long lunch. He'd made me admit another woman who had gone off her meds. She was screaming in the intake room, off her chair, on the floor, in the corner, because at home she had a new little baby, and she had just been told her stay with us would be indefinite. Why had that made me cry? The deaths didn't do that to me. So often, in fact, I was happy to see them off. There was a man with a big belly of ascites, the fluids that gather once your liver has failed. And we kept the surgeons away from him, despite a problem with his heart, because he had shouted and growled he'd for fuck's sake had enough. When we gave him the drip that took away his breathlessness, the morphine, I felt, as I rarely did, that we had done a good thing. But this brought me to tears: a woman in a room drawing shapes on the floor, saying, I can be better, I can be better, I promise to be better if you just let me go.

There is a story about my mother, about her first pregnancy, a daughter she miscarried. The story— like any old ghost story, it was told only late at night—went that when my mother was eight months pregnant, she went in for a checkup and the doctor couldn't find the heartbeat. The doctors wanted to induce labor, but my mother refused and instead risked sepsis to carry the fetus to term. A few weeks later, the baby was born dead and rotten and black. And my father was the one who told us this story over and over, a story about grief, about risk without reward. The climax, in his telling, was his horror at seeing the child like that, posed in a crib in a blanket.

A lot of people were dying of the flu that year. You didn't see it on the news but it was a chill in the air for a few of us who worried or cared directly for the patients who lost their toes and fingers. The treatment did that, the heart and lung machine. They call it dry gangrene. When you're young enough, strong enough, the overblown immune response floods your lungs and kills you. But you don't need lungs to live in a place like this hospital. They have a machine that is lungs and a heart in itself. It's crude to look at, the huge-bore hoses, the buckets and pumps. It looks more fit for mixing paint. And though it can keep the torso warm and oxygenate the brain, it lacks the strength or subtlety to make it all the way out to the extremities, so they grow blue and ache, then numb as the nerves dry, then shrivel and blacken and fall off on their own. When patients are on these machines, you can't hear the heartbeat, only a pulseless roar in the place the beat should be.

I lose track, sometimes, of why I am telling you all of this. Not to be upsetting, believe me, please. A scrap from someplace, quoted someplace else: I don't want to be listened to. I want to be believed.

Ada, in her first bed, in the time of the quiet fever. We'd held off the seizures, but things had begun going wrong. The doctors tried not to worry. Most likely, they said, delirium from waiting like she was, kept inside so long. But she was disappearing a little at a time. I'd ask her questions, the basics: Where is your house? What was your lunch? And she would give some answer, sure as ever, with the husband slowly shaking his head behind her. Well, it was fruit, at least, she almost shouted. But she still knew her name and could repeat *Today is a sunny day.* Even at night, when the drugs for sleep kicked in, I'd still come in and check her lines, look out the window for any signs, and see nothing but the stopped little boat.

The way she disappeared was subtle at first. If you asked only stock questions, you'd never even notice. She could do hello, how are you, are you in any pain? But the thread bent to breaking if you asked her to invent something. Tell me a story, I said one day. A story? she asked. Sure, I said. Just some made-up thing. All right, she said. Once upon a time. And then she stalled and started again. Once upon a time, there was a man. She stalled. And the man was—she looked straight ahead with a thoughtful face, not stern, but like a child at a puzzle. And the man was fractured? She shook her head. She said, I'm not telling it right. And then she was quiet. Empty speech, the neurologists call it. She can speak, but she can't say anything.

There was still time to do the busywork I liked. I brought warm blankets around a lot or went off to find for a certain patient a certain kind of muffin. I tried to play music for anyone dying alone, though it was always a tough guess what might be the best genre. I asked the families from time to time, but it seemed that they would lie to me. I saw a lot of sons grimacing at the stiff hymns and spirituals their mothers swore they loved and wondered if they might like something sharper. One man left alone had been a singer himself, the lead in a family band that performed in the style of somebody else. On short notice I could find only their Christmas album. It got a lot of laughs, "Good King Wenceslas" in a dying man's room in the middle of a city summer. He had a beautiful voice, at least, and didn't grimace at all.

People will surprise you with how much they can stand up to. The poor more than the rich, is my experience. More poor people laugh at death or tell you they saw the ghost of their brother in the hallway saying, Come on with me when you're ready, I'm holding the door. You could guess they have more peace because they have suffered already enough. When you are poor, you can't pretend you don't need your community. The seminarian told me that, or close enough. He gave me a scarf once, wide and cashmere, in the bland checkered beiges I am fond of. And I thought he would approve when I gave it to a woman who was cold on the street. He acted touched, but what he did was run out later, find her, buy the scarf back, and give it to me again. I asked what he had paid for it. *Not enough* is what he said.

Whenever a binge put our mother down for the count, we children had the run of the house. We overflowed the sinks, lit tissues into glowing ghosts that burned up before they hit the carpet. It was only at night that the fear crept in, the cold sense that we weren't being tended. We were still children when the towers fell. Our mother sat cross-legged on the floor and watched the scenes on repeat for weeks. I would dream constantly of machines falling from the sky. In a bed shared with one of the little ones, a sister, I would lie awake at night, smelling her doggish child smell and listening in the dark, then grab her if a plane flew low and run out into the yard.

Family of Origin

I think a lot about what I have been spared, slights and pains and violences that someone else, by weight or worth roughly indistinguishable from me, has not. There is a Catholic theodicy concerning suffering: that it is universally finite, that the suffering of someone is de facto lessened if someone else can suffer more. Some cancer patients act this out, bravely declining analgesics. But I have no reason to think this is true.

The cancer hospitals are in every case gleaming, though you still can't buy your way out of one. Cancer, that great specter, the disease of no one's fault. Except lung, of course—how rough that must be for the nonsmokers, how often they must want to hold up their blamelessness. I'd probably put it on a

T-shirt if it happened to me, if it were true: NEVER SMOKER. Drinkers get their hepatocellular carcinomas and cancers of the stomach and the head and neck. Is it her fault? the sister of a patient with cirrhosis and newly diagnosed liver cancer asked a young doctor to whom I was assigned. What is the answer to a question like that? The doctor picked a good one. She said, Why do you ask?

The illnesses in my family are all like these, those that appear to be diseases of volition, or the diseases of trauma that are their sequelae. Oh, I had a grandfather with a bad heart, but I don't know in what way. Not, at least, from the perspective of cardiology. I know the pills he was prescribed were a kind that kill you if you take them by the handful, which he did when my mother was barely driving age. I know his face from an oil painting and from the small pale eyes and square jaws he left on the faces of my mother and all of her siblings and all of my brothers as well. The girls in my generation all look like our fathers.

The portrait stayed up even after the suicide, and my grandmother spent a year in bed and came out Roman Catholic. There is a line from that portrait to where I am now and where I am going, up and out of this first-generation poverty. We were only tourists in the poor people's grocery store, where you had to deposit a quarter to free a cart from where they're all chained together in the front. Our lives were a rebellion on my mother's part, so deep and ill-aimed it could only have been mental illness. When we showed up for a rare visit to my father's house, in dirty clothing, with head lice, with no clear habits of dental hygiene, he railed at us: Is this the way you live with your mother? He was the father of just us first few. He taught us the math of payroll deductions for child support, taught us the word *whore* and that our mother was one. He called the boys fags because they never learned to ride bikes.

I meet men like him wherever I go, work with them and for them, though I have with time learned not to date them. He was also a disgrace to a rich family, a college dropout doing blue-collar work for a utilities company, but his house had a fireplace and top sheets on the beds, and on the rare weekends he would have us to see him, he would stay up late drinking and let us watch adult television. His father, a man I met only once, had an airplane in his garage, an in-ground pool in his rolling green yard. That day he gave check-book covers and plastic wristwatches to me and my brothers as gifts.

The next father was a bodybuilder, the next baby another boy. The father had a small side business involving VHS players, stacked atop one another, for copying the tapes from the video store. He watched action and horror day and night and did not try to keep us from seeing the blood and bodies. He would tell us about the boys cut up under John Wayne Gacy's floorboards and then send one of us on an errand in the basement and have some brother hold the door closed until the crying stopped. Next after that was the slaughterhouse man, who walked the house in his boots late into the night and beat my brothers with an extension cord.

When I first started writing, this was what I wrote. Grotesque, my classmates called it, prohibitively dark. It doesn't matter just because it happened, someone told me more than once. But that's not true; I know that now. It matters most because it happened, if you learn to tell it right. You learn to leave things out until truth is what it sounds like.

My mother through all this was in the kitchen or

on the back porch with a cigarette or sitting on the sofa eating ice from a cup and watching true-crime television. I know what girls like you do, she would sometimes say to me if I left the house in the evening. For a long time, I believed she could see inside of me, that she knew things about me I did not. But I was innocuous, at least back then, terrified of vice and its consequences.

The last of the fathers was a doctor, it's true. By this time, I was in high school. He would see my mother in his second house, a house he paid me to clean, a house where he could do the things he needed to hide from his family. He drove a red car with a soft taupe top. He never left his wife, of course, though this was what my mother held out for. Once he and I were alone together in her bedroom. I was twelve and packing a bag so he could take her to an out-of-town rehab. He asked if I had ever heard of pregnancy entrapment. My mother had quit her job, enrolled in school to be a nurse. She will call all this the great love of her life.

In the neurology clinic, a shadow again. All of the patients presented with headaches. I saw them alone and then did an exam. As they spoke, I wrote the story in my head better than they told it, sharpened to make my point when I presented it to the attending. One had been started on a new medication. She was sleeping better, I reported to her doctor. He was ardent but a little off. Ask her about her dreams, he said. Dreams, he said, are a side effect. Together we returned to the patient's room. She began again, talking about her pain, how it affected her, her family, her work. But do you have vivid dreams? he asked her. She didn't even pause. Yes, she said. I do. I always have. I always dream about my mother. Even before the medication, he said, disappointed. Yes, she said, even before.

And the drug wasn't working, anyway; she was still having headaches every day. She was having a hard time getting out of bed. *Failing the medication* is what we call this.

June used to have the same dream all the time as a kid, that she was being chased by an animal, something vague and large-toothed and salivating. When the monster caught her, it would pull off its head, which was a large plush mask like a mascot wears. It was always her mother inside, she said, and we both agreed this was a little on the nose. But it was her father, she told me eventually, who some late nights would come crawling into her bed.

A joke from somewhere. The patient comes in complaining of pain, ten out of ten—ten means the worst you can imagine. The doctor says she must be seeking attention. Yes, she says. Medical attention.

Modified Trauma

Mother, father, little wife, a congress of aunts and uncles—they filled the small room off the ICU where we held the difficult conversations. QUIET ROOM was the label on the one off the emergency department, but this one doubled as a conference room and often held the stale smell of leftover lecture takeout. Their relative, an adult, had crashed a car into a tree and was brain-dead. This was the meeting where we broke the news. The young attending spoke of the heroic work we'd done. He said a lot about the salts, the chemistries, about how we had gotten the values back to where they should be. This was not a treatment, just part of the routine required to make a declaration of brain death. But his long-winded and technical talk had accidentally given the family hope, so after the doctor laid out what was gone, even the patient's drive to draw breath, the family leaped back to the sodium test. But the salts are good now, the levels are set? This was the father, at the table's end, his hands gripped together to smother the shaking. And the doctor began again, from the beginning, chemistries and lines, tests and imaging, the whole dark flood of technicalities. I stopped him. What we are trying to say is that your son is already dead. And we're sorry, I tried to add, but the sobbing room was deaf.

Death, in the hospital, means certain functions of the body cease irreversibly. When permanence defines an event, it can be difficult to mark the point when it has actually occurred. In truth, nothing except death can be defined by its permanence, since being dead is the only thing any of us will ever permanently do. Arguable, notes the seminarian.

Brain death is death, they teach us in medical school. But unlike conventional, layman's death, this kind had to be invented. In the 1950s, the iron lung was replaced by positive pressure administered through a tube going from the mouth to the lungs. This method was safer, more effective, and it quickly led to a proliferation of ventilated patients in permanent comas.

A Catholic anesthesiologist, troubled by the implications, asked the pope if these breathing machines could be turned off in cases that were clearly hopeless. The pope said yes, with a tough caveat: As long as the soul has left the body. There is no serum test or vital sign to measure *exitus animae*.

A committee at Harvard wrote the criteria for brain death in 1968, the year after the first successful human heart transplant. The heart, notably, was once considered the seat of the soul, then Descartes relocated it to the pineal gland, one of the only unpaired structures in the brain, and then it was done away with entirely. The recipient of this heart, a white South African, died eighteen days later of an infection caused by medications the donor heart required, but the new heart had functioned normally until his death. An early draft of the Harvard statement did note: "There is great need for the tissues and organs of the hopelessly comatose in order to restore to health those who are still salvageable." So a new form of death was invented. It is not wholly ingenuous to present the Harvard definition as a biologic fact. For this reason, doctors are taught not to engage families in the specifics of brain death, which rightly may serve to confuse them. Organ donation, it is vital to note, saves thousands of lives every year.

And we have to agree on the words for things. Because if brain death weren't death, not really, and we took necessary organs out of people while they were alive, we would have to admit that there are lives that are unsalvageable, or hopeless, or inherently worth less than others. And what would it mean to admit that?

Stay honest if you can. That was the last thing he said to me, Ada's husband, the day he left for good, the day I walked him with all his bags of blankets and books and family photographs from the bedside to the elevator bank and held him a little as he cried.

Let me go back. One interesting fact is this meeting about the brain-dead son, it took place under interpretation. So every statement, every list of study results, took twice as long and gave us a long time to look at all their faces, the family's, and think about what we were complicit in. And what we saw, those of us who were looking, was an insane and indelible thing—the long light wait before so many lives were stained forever. The other bit I left out is that in the grief that followed what I said, the father paused to pose a question, interpreted as: How did it end? And the doctor began an explanation of the effects of swelling on the brain stem, which the interpreter, with a pained face, dutifully repeated. But how did it end? the father asked again. Without pain, I said. A shot in the dark. And true enough, we can all hope, together.

The doctor caught me in the hall. Bold, he said. I like it.

There is a whole subfield of study that covers the trauma of being a medical interpreter, of being in that room and putting those awful words into your mouth, tearing whole worlds down. Ours was crying afterward, discreetly in the hall. I asked her how she did it. Whatever your crutch, she said, you lean on it heavily. I thought of the seminarian. I had started calling him Esteban, although that wasn't his name. From a story I read he reminded me of. He was the handsomest drowned man in the world.

A man in his thirties, a flu survivor, now without hands or feet. He had a hole in his neck for a tube to breathe through. This far out, his biggest problem was anxiety. He described, in gasps, since he was new to the valve that allowed him to speak, the trauma of the flash flood in his lungs, of losing his ability to breathe. And now he jolted and wept at the sound of every ambulance, as triggered as Little Albert with the rat. He hadn't even seen the places where his hands and feet should have been. We kept them covered in soft cloth, taught him hands-free sudoku and deep-breathing techniques.

Physical Exam

In the town where I grew up, I was often asked by store clerks and hairdressers where I was from. Not the way the Texan had been asked; I have always had a soft Caucasian Middle American appearance. It was about the way I spoke. My mother had what I later learned to call a transatlantic accent—*again* rhymed with *pain*—that morphed into a Midwestern twang only after I left for college. And half my words I learned from books and didn't know how to pronounce. Even after college and into medical school, I sounded like English was my second language, June and the Texan said.

Words weren't all I picked up from books. The cigarettes, for one example, were straight from between the fingers of Salinger women lounging wanly beside telephones. And I got ideas from teen magazines I never could have invented: that you can use your fingers to induce vomiting or cut yourself with razor blades in the event of unbearable suffering. I tried this in high school, along the lines of my hands—to hide it, to try to avoid lasting consequences. Years later, at a street fair, a palm reader called me out. These are just scars, she said, with a tone of soft disgust. But she gave me a fortune regardless: Try to make some money of your own.

An early memory of being a young participant in a welfare scam. We were brought to this woman's house—I think her name was Delores—my brothers and I, and with her own little daughter and a few other kids, she claimed a clan of nearly eleven. And who came was something like the state inspector for welfare, and the host was one of my mother's boyfriends. He said: This is my wife, and these are my children. Later we got a cut of shipment food from the government, everything canned, with white stark labels in a plain serifed font that said MIXED FRUIT or CORN or RED SAUCE. The woman's real daughter, she had only one, taught me you could eat the small yellow flowers that grew up in the cracks of the sidewalk.

Not as food, but because it was fun, a chance to take the world at large and put it in your mouth.

Weren't you ashamed? This was the country-house kid, the odd man out in anatomy class. We were studying together the nerves and bones of the hand and arm. Not beside the body, in the lab, but from books, out in the sun. He was tutoring me, trying to get me to carry my weight. We had gotten to talking about how we had arrived here, he from an Ivy League, of course. Having started early, he was the youngest in our class. I'd told him—I often say too much—how in my application essay I wrote about being poor, about growing up the way I did and never seeing doctors. I am still afraid when a fever or a long cough or a burning when I pee forces me to the health center. I can't get used to letting people touch me. But during the interview, no, shame had not occurred to me. Before I'd said a word, the doctor sent to judge me told a long story about a brother she had who was born with that thalidomide body, with crab-claw hands and nearly no legs, standing less than a table's height full grown. Although she was the daughter of a very rich man and had never known a poor kid's want, it had hurt her so much to see her brother suffer, it placed her apart from the world forever, and in that way she ended up in psychiatry. She said, I know how it feels to protect someone. But who did she think I was protecting?

When I ask my mother about the past, she refuses to answer, or, when she is feeling more generous, she states she does not remember. I have, though, a light touch of prosopagnosia, face-blindness, and from this I lightly deduce I was not shown many faces as an infant. As a child lying in bed at night, I realized I could not call faces into my mind, or I could, but only as pieces, only one feature at a time. They would shift and pulse when I tried to assemble them. I can sometimes remember a face only exactly as it appears in a photograph that I own personally and have studied over time. Still, I was cared for enough to live and breathe, and that is plenty.

I wonder, though—do you know a face if you know it only as a photograph? I read a philosopher once who railed against the projected world of perspective drawing, where you align all the edges of things to a single point in the infinite distance. This is considered realism, but in what way is this realistic? These landscapes, he said, have an air of decency, remain at a distance, do not involve or require the viewer. But this is not how the world appears when we encounter it in perception.

This controls the movement of their unfolding, he said, yet kills their trembling life.

We ran into the woman from the welfare scam a decade later, my mother and I. We were buying food at the poor people's grocery store. She had grown obese and looked pained just by walking and looked aged awfully from the smoking I supposed she did all day. She or my mother nodded and the other nodded back. They knew each other from AA, so the rule was to keep quiet. Her daughter just died, my mother said when the woman was out of earshot. Her daughter was two years older than me, so sixteen at the time of this story. She had hanged herself in a closet. I remembered the way she had taught me to tie flat sheets high on the trunks of trees and make hammocks to rest on in the unrelenting sun, despite the traffic on their two-laned street and what the drivers would think, the two of us eating flowers from the sidewalk cracks and sleeping up in the trees.

That last time my mother was pregnant, the time with the doctor, I came home one day to find her sitting on the dining-room floor. There was a gun in her hand, that big square gun that shoots staples into the wall, the one we used to tack plastic over the broken windows. She didn't look up. She was shooting staples into her arm, making her way from elbow to wrist, unflinching with the sharp shots, ticks like marking time.

Reverence is almost certainly wrongheaded, but I have never believed in suicide as a moral failure. In medical school, we learned suicide as the end stage of a specific illness and not at all a serious question of philosophy. I think a lot about one attending on a crowded hepatology service who sighed to himself constantly, audibly: Oh, kill me. Oh, slit my wrists with a knife.

If you get short of breath and find yourself wanting to explain the sodium again, looking away from a mother whose son is brain-dead, try to remember that you are afraid, and remember where the fear comes from. Not from this, not from the particulars of what your mother did or didn't do or how she stood, drunk, in the frozen-foods aisle of the poor people's grocery store flicking a lighter until an old man said, Ma'am, you are lighting the wrong end of a cigarette.

Don't settle on the smallest story you can live with. We all hurt, hurt in the bones, have hurt for each other since the day we were born. Best not blame our mothers for it.

How would you do it? the therapist asked. Now I know what not to say. Back then, I had roof rights on a six-floor walk-up and said so. That's how you get committed, a three-day hold for wanting to and saying it out loud. What else can I say about that place, that room, that I haven't said already? The TV, the armed guard, the woman who didn't speak English and didn't get spoken to, the way she cried and cried. When someone asked if I had a history of abuse, I told them all about it. And for all that, all I got was an appointment to enroll in a research study.

The interview was nearly over when I asked the psychiatrist if we should talk about my qualifications for medical school. No, she said. You are already accepted. I think what she saw in me was a trait we must have shared, a knowing, in our bones, how easily our lives could have been different. Still, I hear my classmate ask, Weren't you ashamed?

Extraordinary Measures

A mystery writer—I am trying to remember her name. Someone did a study after she died, a study of the books she had written. She had dementia, Alzheimer's, maybe, and the study showed that far before she was demented outright, her books began to contain less specificity. Words like *things* began appearing everywhere; settings grew more and more vague, like a world fogged over with cataracts, like pages soaked with bleach. A teacher I once had was not fond of similes. She said nothing really is like anything else, described a church as being as quiet as a church. What would a hospital be? Not sterile, no, not remotely clean. It is safer to jump off a cliff than to be hospitalized. With a parachute on, I mean.

Churches are quiet, true enough. Old and cold

and safe. There was one hidden in the hospital that I had never noticed until Esteban showed me. It was easy to miss. Newer additions had been built up all around it, swallowing its outline completely. It was round with old wood and dark bricks, stained-glass windows with boards behind them so light could not shine through. I didn't know what happened there, but signs said everyone was welcome. FIND COMFORT HERE, said a paper taped to the wall, BUT DO NOT SLEEP OR EAT!

In the emergency department, the notes wrote themselves. All you did on the screen was click some boxes. The output, for example, for a patient intubated after an overdose read:

This is a new problem.

The current episode started two hours ago.

The problem occurs rarely.

The problem has not changed since onset.

Nothing aggravates the symptoms.

Nothing relieves the symptoms.

She has tried nothing.

Esteban said we don't do things because of what we believe in, but we come to believe in what we are doing. He was glowing in a stoned way, just having come from a service where the churchgoers lined up and he and a priest, a woman priest in a plain white robe, used warm water and soft cloths and washed and dried, one by one, everybody's feet. He floated around like that for weeks after, with a glow in his eyes and a glow that you could almost see coming off his hands. He would walk around my little room blessing the books and the furnishings.

He was teaching me to pray, in a joking way: Give me good digestion, Lord, and something to digest. He told me a story about a missionary in a jungle who found a flipped truck by the dirt road with a man inside, crushed almost to death. He ran to pray with him before the man's last breath, and the man became quite angry. He yelled at the missionary. I imagined his voice muffled in the wetness of the jungle air, imagined the blood on his body, his face. Don't try to save my soul, he said to the missionary. Please, just save my life.

Ada. I didn't tell you she had a daughter. She was that age between childhood and teenage that it is almost rude to look at directly. She didn't come around much before the coma, when her father still thought this was something she could be kept out of. He was plagued, the husband, by the tube in

Ada's mouth, the one she needed now to breathe. He couldn't remember the last thing she said before they put it in there. As she grew confused, she had gotten angrier, even at him, biting at him, slapping cups of juice from his hands. *It was fruit, at least* was the last thing she ever said to me. We didn't really know each other very well at all.

People have told me things I refuse to believe: All crying is crying selfishly. If you can't explain it, you don't know what it means.

Esteban came from a bad-hearted family. The men all died, or tried to, in their forties. His own father had gone out like that, alone in the den, watching late-night television, when Esteban was seventeen. All he remembers is the lights along the walls when the ambulance came and staring into a candy dish, some old awful hard candy no one ever ate. And his mother rode with the paramedics to the hospital with his father in the back, already growing cold. Eventually it dawned on him that he would have to go get her. That he should bring something. But he couldn't think of what, so he brought a blanket he could wrap her up in, his little mother, like they do after trauma in a movie.

In a few short years, when I am almost through with residency, I will see my father dead—all our fathers die of heart attacks. I will come alone to bury him, and in the box when I see him, I will touch his hand and feel no abjection. I will feel only love, or something I want to be love, which will feel like fear but will not be fear. Words will circle this place and fail to find it.

Oh, kill yourself. My father used to say that. I cried a lot and what it did was make him angry. He called me psychically frail. For a short time after he died, I thought to myself: Now none of this will change, none of this will ever be different. This was a thought about death, but it had been true already. It already would never have been different.

These were the women from patient services, three at least, each standing about six feet tall, giants in suits with skirts. They were here to make Ada's family leave. The rule is you can sit with the body for four hours tops, then it must be rolled down to the morgue, by order of the health department. I had not known Ada had so many siblings. But it was her daughter who wouldn't let go of her hand. It's time to get them out of here, the tallest woman said, look at her.

I did.

Once, for my birthday, some of my brothers offered to dig up a cat of mine that was dead. A car had hit it in the spring, and we buried it out in the yard, out past the lilacs, in a grocery bag. Now it was fall and I was turning ten. The ground was still soft. I was a good sport, a tagalong, always up for a challenge to my fake little bravery. All right, I said. It took a thousand tries until we found the right spot and dug deep enough. I remember seeing the knotted handles, the stiff ungivingness of the bag as my brothers began to pull it up. Don't, I said. Stop. And those awful brothers, who would chase me with live snakes through the yard, who would sneak into my room at night and hide old meat under my bed, for the only time in their whole lives did what I said, and we put the dirt back over the cat together.

Okay, all right. Esteban's father didn't grow cold in the ambulance. They got him back. The surgeons took huge vessels from both of his legs and gave his heart blood again. But he did stare, Esteban, into the candy dish. Eventually it dawned on him he would have to go and see him. That he should bring something. He couldn't think of what, so he brought a toothbrush in hopes there would be reason to stay the night. And the father recovered fully, and they celebrate it every year like a birthday, with balloons and colorful crepe and cake, the whole nine yards. And who would lie about a thing like that?

That cat. It, he, could not be kept away from me. I had to close him in a drawer at night if I wanted to get any sleep. And I have a memory of sitting on the cracked back steps crying, having suffered a small, now unrecalled household indignity, and the cat kept coming up to me, up the steps, rubbing his head on my feet and legs and against my still hands as if to make me pet him. I tossed him off the steps but he just kept coming back, even when I threw him down harder and harder.

I'm sorry, that's a thick one. I even thought so at the time. The cat was acting like a poem, and then he went and died. But life does that, so much sometimes it's embarrassing to talk about it. The day before my first board exam I got some kind of gastroenteritis, and as I was suffering cramps and diarrhea in my cold little room, panicked, fever-dreaming, seeing faces in the tiles on the ceiling, workmen came to the door and said the toilet was broken. They unbolted it from the floor, propped it on a hand truck, and rolled it away. I passed that exam, though. I'm very good at barely getting by.

Georg Groddeck, the father of psychosomatic medicine, would say to a patient with a broken leg, after setting the leg and prescribing exercises and giving a massage and prohibiting excess of food or drink: Why did you break your leg, you yourself?

A convention of English grammar, too, is that the patient is the subject, not the object, of illness or ailment: I got sick; I broke my leg. The experience of illness, of something like gastroenteritis, is certainly that it comes to you, appears in your body unwilled and unwanted. But what you have to say is *I got sick,* in the same way you would say *I got breakfast;* you went out looking for this and obtained it and brought it back. And studies show that, in contrast to speakers of languages with other grammars, English speakers are more likely to assign blame to the person present in an accident and demand from them redress.

The alternative—illness as something that visits itself upon you—is consistent with germ theory and a great way to shake off metaphor. But illness as something we have sought, have earned, harsh as it may sound, retains for us a sense of control, volition. Anyway, doctors hate being told how to say things.

Esteban asked if I would come see him preach. I told him I liked churches only when they were empty. But he set me up in the back row, behind a few pews of West Indian ladies in vivid little hats. His sermon was about what it meant that Jesus had a body. Like this: If you were deeply in love and you were seeing your beloved off on a steamship somewhere at a dock, you would want every moment, to hold it, draw out every last second. But if you also had to take a shit, you would be miserable instantly, dying at once for that boat and your beloved to hurry up and leave. Those aren't the words exactly. I do think he meant that we are wholly subject to our bodies, in all their gross immediacy. It made the churchwomen blush. And it was the first time I ever thought of a Jesus who would have to use the bathroom. I imagined Jesus in my little room with the toilet just taken away. So he has to run, run down the hall, past the doors of all his classmates, the pain in his gut making a white-hot burn all the way up to his teeth, and the pain made worse by his being so exposed, so close to losing stool in a public place. Humiliation—is *human* hidden in the root of that word? It comes up so much in humanity.

After the sermon, everyone lined up for communion. The priest muttered something about Christ and heaven before he set the little wafer in each mouth. Esteban followed, in his robes, with a chalice. In the early church, he told me, the words they said when they gave the bread were *Believe what you see and become who you are.*

Another time I met him there just after he had set up a funeral. The mourners had not yet arrived, but the body was ready, a woman all painted in a wide-open box. I thought once, when I was college-aged, that the worst part of dying would be that you couldn't tell anyone about it. Because all I want to do with a scene like this, this woman in a box, is describe it to somebody. He was surprised by the way I stared. Nothing you haven't seen before, he said gently. But never one like this. She was so done up, the colors all just off, uncanny, surreal. So far from the ones with holes in their throats, the bruises and tubes, the hoses. The woman in the box seemed pleasantly abstract, at peace with her own vacancy.

A poet who had lost her husband said he would

come to her in dreams. But all he ever said was *Am I really dead? Really?*

The machines. We can keep up a life with no hope of living, and we do, despite what it costs. The nurses pay, mostly, the ones who tend these bodies, keep them clean. We had one so ill and thin, his skin was coming off in sheets, and he had to be loaded on every analgesic, all the way to top-dose ketamine, and still he groaned when touched however gently. He was rotting alive, dying of tuberculosis. The staff tried not to see him. He couldn't even close his eyes, and the whites were thick with scratches and the irises sunken in, in spite of the petroleum jelly we kept them covered with. His wife said the whole thing was up to God. If God wanted him to die, he would not keep living. In medicine, said the ethics man, the F-word is *futility*.

There was an elevator in the subway station nearest to the hospital, the only way up from the tracks to ground level, in which it was rumored a student once contracted tuberculosis. We were taught by upperclassmen to call it the tuberculator. It is normal to laugh at the things that scare you, but tuberculosis was not something we were particularly afraid of.

At our hospital, TB was a disease of immigrants and prisoners—is this who we were laughing at? The elevator, it's true, pressed you in close to a lot of poor people's bodies.

Historically, tuberculosis evokes not poverty but the romance of poets, of leisure, retreat, and a long list of artists who died of it: Keats, Kafka, Chopin. Tuberculosis for a long time remained definitively mysterious in a field that prizes certainty above all else. It provokes an old, epigenetic dread. But a quarter of everyone on earth has latent tuberculosis right at this moment. It still kills more than a million people a year. It's hard for me to guess if you know this already. The further I go, the less I know what's supposed to be common knowledge.

Sontag contrasts the pure, radiant tuberculosis patient with the erasure of self seen in crowded, environmental diseases like cholera—another treatable illness that kills thousands of people, elsewhere, every year. Erasure was the part of plague that terrified me most as a child: being subsumed in a large-scale catastrophe, being buried in a mass grave, being wholly undifferentiated. Something about the school provoked a similar anxiety. It seemed to prize, as

June once put it, extraordinary normality, studied un-originality, and a violent dismissal of style.

I would come to the ICU in the morning while outside it was still dark and greet Ada's husband, if he was awake, in the chair by the door where he slept. If he was asleep, I would try to let him stay that way. I would say her name once or twice, no more than a whisper, and watch her not respond. Her body was swelling from the fluids we gave her mixed with all the drugs she had to take, since we were treating her for everything that came into our heads. By the end, her eyes were splitting open at the corners, and serous fluids ran down the sides of her face like tears. What does it mean? the husband would ask. Sad as it was, it didn't mean anything.

Withdrawal of Care

World *without end* is my favorite line to say when I push through a service at Esteban's church. They write it all out for you, with stage directions even, when to stand and when to kneel, when to draw a cross over your head. Even in the darker days, in the dark house, on the wet dark steps in the basement, world without end was what I wanted, more world, more life—I have wanted it in writing that this world would stay, and I could stay here with it.

I didn't know—a lot of people don't—how few patients survive resuscitation, so I would rush to the codes in the emergency department, the one where I volunteered to stock carts and bring blankets, to watch for the miracle. A lot of people were brought in after being found down, meaning they had been alone when their hearts stopped, with no one to time how long they had been without breathing. This is always bad. But they still got the works, got rolled into the trauma bay, got their shocks and chest compressions. On the hopeless cases, those who came in cold, the doctors offered to let me practice. It is true that the ribs break and true that you can hear it. Seventeen percent of them live to leave the hospital. We call these extraordinary measures.

There are signs around the emergency department to prepare us for things you wouldn't want to think about. We need to know what smallpox looks like, anthrax—in a patient, I mean—any illness that could be turned into a weapon. And then the ones that could just become plagues themselves, like the famous black death, which is still around but easily treated, I believe, with doxycycline. Still, there are other fish to fry; a strain of gonorrhea now resists all medication, and a fungus partial to diseased lungs can't be killed by anything. REMEMBER HAND HYGIENE, spout friendly wall signs every few feet.

Some of this is new, but a lot of us were raised on apocalypse. The church and conjoined school I was schooled in, attended, made girls wear dresses, since pants were an offense to Jesus. We learned by heart that the wages of sin were death. Even worse somehow than the fires of hell, more fearsome, to me, was the Rapture. I would wake from nightmares and check the beds. The youngest children, it was said, were called up automatically, but I didn't know the cutoff age and worried for a brother, the bodybuilder's son, who was already coming out rough, running off and stealing and setting fires, once nearly burning down a neighbor's attached garage. I was afraid it would just be him and me when the Horsemen came to fell the cities.

How did that first life, that childhood, end? Hard to say how, and hard to say when. But I can tell you how I got out of town. Every book I read said you had to go to the city to see what the world really was. I applied to one college and I got in. In that interstitium, when I knew I was leaving but hadn't yet gone, I felt for sure that I would die, because getting out was harder to imagine than being dead.

My first place in the city was in an old hotel. I shared a room with a Korean design student who cried when I left the door unlocked until she learned to lock me out. I lived in rented rooms where I could get them, with crust punks and arts queers and boyfriends when I could keep them. I held jobs while I could and when I had to. I worked at a French restaurant that never closed, so small and tightly tabled that at night when I lay down to sleep, I would spin and spin from all the turning. The place had regulars there like in the novel I wanted my life to be: an opera singer's opera-singer son, who had a designated table and drank milked coffee out of an enormous bowl; a trust-fund nobody in middle age always taking fistfuls of vitamins over his egg-white omelet. After shift I would sit sometimes at the bar with the wine they served to the teenagers on staff—the real adults, in contrast, did cocaine in the basement—and the trust-fund man would join me some nights and give unsolicited advice on my grammar. He'd noticed, for instance, that I called the floor *the ground,* that I started answers to questions by saying *The reason is because.* He said I was otherwise well-spoken for a service worker, and he took me out once to a private club where they kept in a frame the note that Edwin Booth wrote after his brother killed President Lincoln. I didn't know what all of this was or what it was supposed to mean. I just wanted to be somebody.

This was college, and then graduate school—the natural sequela of studying the liberal arts. I was buying time, living on student loans. In Brooklyn once I had a roommate who reminded me of one of my better brothers, and we stayed up late a lot, smoking weed and petting his cat, until one night he told me that he had been accused of raping a girl when he was a student at Cornell. He had been drinking, they both had, it was hard to say. It ruined my life, he said. Socially, he meant, because he stayed in school and kept his scholarship and graduated. He was in law school now. He wanted me to feel for him. Why do people like to tell me the worst things they've ever done? Or a secret is something you tell only one person at a time. Like the Texan once, late into a late night, confessing that in Thailand on vacation he slept with a child prostitute. I think she was a child, he said. She really could have been one.

When you walk the hospital with the hospice doctors, the others sometimes call you the death squad. Not just the surgeons with their eye for statistics, but doctors and nurses of other traditions who oppose the team's perceived hopelessness on moral or religious grounds. I'm guessing that. It is hard to understand. In the back ICU where that patient died strapped to his bed, there was a nurse who had clearly had enough of the hospice doctors. She tried to keep us away from the families and tried to schedule procedures for when we weren't around, sneaking surgeons to the bedside to place the tubes into stomachs, to push beige bags of nutrition into patients who couldn't eat. It seemed each side believed the other complicit in a form of torture. At least on mine, we asked the families: Who was your father before he was sick? What did he live for? What did he like to eat?

In that unit we had another case, a very old woman whose heart had a bad valve that the surgeons wanted to replace. But now, her daughters felt, her care was getting away from them. I don't think she'll make it through, they told me. Can we take her off these machines? She had leads glued into the mess of her hair, and a tube in her mouth she choked against the rare times she was awake. And the younger doctor privately agreed: she wouldn't make it through the surgery. Will you tell the family? I asked, but he said his boss wouldn't like that. And he wouldn't want to see you here either, he told me. But I did come back, to see the daughters by her bed and to talk to them.

I can't think of a thing I did to help except tell them how to notice if their mother was in pain. I showed them the kinds of faces she might make, acted out the possible restlessness. The nurses never wanted to give dying patients morphine. They seemed to believe that morphine was fatal and didn't want it falling to them to have killed somebody. Do all the lies we tell ourselves concern the cost of things?

The same pope who approved withdrawing ventilators from those whose souls had departed approved the principle of dual effect, which permits hastening death with sedatives and pain medications as long as hastening death is not the primary intention. Of course not everyone can abide such subtlety.

The protesters held signs that read DOCTORS CAN BE WRONG. This was on the national news. A child, a girl in middle school, had bled out after a routine tonsillectomy. Her heart stopped, and by the time they got her back, she was brain-dead. Something else unique to brain death—the family is allowed to object to the designation. For this reason, in this hospital, we don't even perform brain-death testing on Orthodox Jewish patients, who consider the breathing body sacredly alive regardless of its brain-stem reflexes. But the girl was not in a state that accommodated her family's objection, so she was transferred by helicopter to a state that did before her doctors could disconnect the ventilator. She died for the first time in California and then died again in New Jersey four and a half years later.

It remains a subject of hot debate, whether she was dead and then recovered, had been misdiagnosed as dead, or was dead throughout the whole ordeal. In the interval between deaths, she did begin menstruating and, according to her family and more than fifty video recordings, began to move her limbs to verbal command. Skeptics called these movements reflexive spinal myoclonus.

Ada was gone a long time before she finally left. Every morning when I came in, I whispered her name and watched her not respond. Next, I took a sharp knuckle and rubbed it on her breastbone. I grabbed the soft skin and muscle above the clavicle and twisted it in a pinch. Lo siento. She didn't flinch. I opened her eyes, one at a time, and shined a light to see if her pupils would constrict, and they did, but less and less. Then I took the tube we used to suction the mucus from her throat and pushed it down to gag her. Not the smallest cough. The husband saw this ritual but rarely asked questions. I had already told him that this was how we look for brain death. The other tests were worse than this, but since she still had reactive pupils, we hadn't done them yet.

I'd learned at last what *lo siento* meant. Not *I'm sorry* exactly, but something more like *I feel you.* And that was all I did. The husband, I would often ask what I could do for him. There wasn't anything. He mostly seemed to want me to sit and talk about life before, or sometimes he would just start up and review the case from the beginning.

The endless, endless tests we took included a few soft-skills questions. For example:

A physician is sad because he has to inform a patient of recent test results that indicate progression of a carcinoma to the terminal phase. When the patient sees the physician's face, he begins to cry and says, It's bad news, isn't it? Which of the following responses by the physician is most appropriate?

A. How have you been since the last time I saw you?
B. Look on the bright side of things.
C. Tell me how you are feeling.
D. Yes.

One day in anatomy we had just cut the sternum from the ribs with a remarkable saw that buzzes at a frequency such that it can cut only bone. You can hold it to your wrist and it won't make even a scratch. So the sternum popped off like the lid of a box, and the heart sat below it in a tough little sac. We took the heart out and were passing it among ourselves, locating the arteries and veins preserved by a rubbery substance the body is pumped with before it gets to us, marveling, or I was, more than a little dazed. Then the professor jumped up, interrupting us. We had a special guest. It was a heart surgeon who daylighted as a talk-show host, telling his fat and faithful daytime audience how to cut cellulite with turmeric and jojoba oil. He was there to tell us the story of his life.

The class lined up for pictures with him afterward, the hearts all abandoned near the bodies they had come in with.

June was not taken in by the TV surgeon. She had a constant quiet posture of dissent that I was half in love with. June had gone to Catholic school and was still friends with some actual nuns. Something would appear in her when she talked about them, some longing for, or fantasy of, self-denial that was not a punishment. I'm making this up, of course, a pretend inner life for a person whose solidity made her hard to read. She wanted, she said, a job where she was allowed to show deep interest in people's souls, and she felt, for some reason, this was psychiatry. A question she asked a lot was: What comes to mind?

Our cadaver's heart was not the first heart we held. We'd looked ahead on another cadaver, the one in the middle of the room that had been fully dissected for us in advance. We called it the perfect body. I had thought it was a woman because of something about the eyes—the lids had been left on although the face was skinned otherwise. The lashes were so long and dark black, in part because the skin had dried and pulled back, but they were curled too, so you knew in life they had been beautiful, and these beautiful teeth, perfect or corrected, left unharmed in the pillage of the rest. I was wrong. He was a man. He had died in his early twenties of an overdose—heroin. His parents were at the ceremony, the memorial for donors I mentioned before. His father said: I wanted you to see my son, and I want you to believe that what he died from is a disease. So his heart was the first I ever held. It was dry and light, the tan tone of dried chicken. And I cried when his father said that. I believed him.

If the doctors cure
then the sun sees it.
If the doctors kill
then the earth hides it.

That poem the dean left for me, what did he want it to mean? I keep it in a drawer. It is so full of threat— is the point that it is written by a patient? I know, of course, that we are all patients eventually.

Show of Force

Proverbs are tested on the neurologic exam. An attending asked a tumor patient: What would it mean if I said a rolling stone gathers no moss? The patient hesitated, then ventured a guess: Don't start shit, won't be shit? This, somehow, was incorrect, despite remaining successfully abstract. The point is to assess comprehension of nonliteral language. The trouble with a test consisting wholly of clichés is that it mostly just measures what people are already familiar with. No sort of brain damage exclusively affects proverb performance. But we learn it, and we put patients through it. A man from Colombia taught me a good one: Don't confuse the shit with the salve.

I can't get a good sense of what it means to live well. The sick poor, you could probably guess, are treated poorly in the hospital. They are more likely to be obese, to be smokers, to suffer a slew of other ills along a social gradient that we attribute, casually, to a failure of will. These disparities in health are especially bad for Black people, though in this cohort, outcomes don't improve much with higher income or more education. Our older lecturers attribute the difference to genetics, perhaps because they have been forbidden from promoting frank eugenics or phrenology. New data suggests that the stress of daily indignity may cause plaque to build up in arteries and lower the birth weight of babies. These, they say, are the social determinants of health.

There was a special pavilion at the hospital for only the especially rich. It had a wide bright lobby with marble floors, a waterfall falling ambiently along a pane of glass, a full grand piano no one ever played. Large tanks of orchids flanked the desk where a man in a suit, a sort of concierge, directed traffic and kept out undesirables. I went there with doctors just a few times on consult, saw the wealthy patients—mostly white, except for a few foreign dignitaries—in satin robes and wrapped in soft, colorful blankets, worrying over menus of gourmet room service. The doctors couldn't help but perform with special reverence in a setup so staged for obeisance. This is the only place you would see attendings searching the halls for cups and water to bring to patients who were thirsty.

A woman in the emergency department in opiate withdrawal. She was writhing, aching, sweating, crying; her bowels turned around in torrents of diarrhea. But it would not kill her. For addicts, there is little sympathy. I asked if I could help, and what she asked for was candy. A fruit kind, please, she said, and patted down the sides of her gown as though she were looking for money. No worries. At the vending machine, nothing fit the bill, only those fat tabs of jelly coated in sugar that made your teeth hurt just to look at, that only a well-meaning grandmother would ever give anyone. But there was nothing else. I brought them to her apologetically. Goddamn! she shouted and sat up, smiling. These are my favorite thing.

The attendings often scolded me for these minor wastes of time. And it's true that the woman left within the hour, against medical advice. The attendings preferred that I stayed useful; for example, chaperoning pelvic exams. Young women, some barely in their teens, would come into the emergency department

113

with sharp pain and strange bleeding, and what they all needed to have ruled out was ectopic pregnancy—when fetal stuff starts growing outside the uterus, a growth that can rupture and kill you. The younger physicians struggled with the ultrasound, a large probe they placed in the vaginal cavity and waved around, while squinting at a grayscale screen that seemed to show nothing but layers of waving lines. They never seemed to mind that the woman was in pain or even crying. In the halls afterward they would joke to each other that girls like these—unspecified, technically, but poor and brown in context—should be sterilized by age thirteen.

What did I say? I said nothing. I held my tongue, and the words went from my mouth down into my body and stayed there until now, repeated for all they are worth. I did wonder how these girls got brought to sex in the first place. It is not uncommon to be raped in this country. The statistic for women is about one in three. So it's her, or it's you, or it's me.

It became apparent—or either way, I began to convince myself—that the fragmentary way my life more and more occurred to me was not a burgeoning mental illness but a product of my training. For example, it was in the nature of our profession for us to constantly approach another person, to attempt to connect, to impress upon them some incarnate lesson (Sir, you must understand that the continued use of intranasal cocaine will lead to strokes, hemorrhages, and eventual death; I see that you are frustrated but I will ask you again not to leave against medical advice), and then walk out, blank-slate your heart for whoever needs you next. There was no lasting emotion, no closure. The work was all notes, no narrative.

Surgery was known to be the worst rotation. There was one surgical subspecialty you could request with lighter hours—breast oncology—but the surgeon who ran it was considered a bit of a creep. Surgeons in general don't try too hard not to be off-putting. They mock the patients they put under (for their belly fat, their scars, their low-class tattoos), mock their students for sweating or shaking or having attended public school. They invite trainees to practice pelvic exams on unconsenting women under sedation. How could any one of them be particularly worse? I was fond of sleeping in.

I was, in fact, sleeping everywhere. Esteban still tried to take me out, when he came down from his grassy hill, to art shows in outer boroughs, but not even avant-garde spectacle, leotard militants dancing up walls, a cross-dressed eighties-style production of *Oedipus Rex* could keep me awake past eight on an off night. I entered new terrain in symptomatic sleep deprivation, from cognitive fog and generalized pain to sudden rage and diarrhea. I could no longer read social cues and would often get lost to little songs playing in my head, upbeat command hallucinations that sometimes concerned jumping out of windows.

It is so clear you are embodied when you are sick and when you are tired. The effect of this chronically, as an education, is to destroy your aptitude for any kind of subtlety. The surgeons get their arrogance from this same well—what they do to their own bodies, the hours, the standing, bent over, the miracle hands. And all that power. There is a strange pipeline of dropout surgeons becoming psychiatrists—this is a story of control.

The breast surgeon immediately required that I give a complete accounting of the chest wall's vascular anatomy. I could not, and so he did, gesturing for each vessel at my chest, his fingers as near as inches. This was a man, you could tell, who knew just where to find the line. It was often just the two of us, if you excluded the scrub nurse, the surgical techs, and the anesthesiologist. The residents clearly tried to avoid him.

The work we did was repetitive. We would remove the breast tissue on one side or both sides, with or without a pearly string of axillary lymph nodes. Sometimes the wounds were left open, and we would leave the place of operation—still called, sometimes, a theater—for the plastic surgeons to come in and perform reconstruction. I preferred it, I found, when we removed both breasts and all the excess flesh and closed the chest flat.

At first, I was allowed only to retract, then graduated to holding the tube that sucked up blood. The surgeon would put his hand over my hand, like this, to tilt it at an angle, and keep it there, as though I were an appliance or something he could drive. What you feel at first is thrilled to be a part of things. But he had other kinds of touching, a hand on the waist, on the small of the back, that lacked the context of patient safety. I don't think I would have had the gall to report him if it hadn't been for the grade he gave me: high pass. He has, the clerkship director explained, strict expectations for assigning honors. I couldn't say it all but did at least mention the hand on the waist. We are, the director said, aware of the problem.

It was odd to enjoy disfiguring women. I said this to June, who had requested general surgery, all guts and gore and awful hours, and loved it. You were treating cancer, she said. We both supposed the prettier students likely got it worse. Do I look like someone who would tell? I asked. She said I looked like someone who would kill him.

What I liked most about June were her manners on the wards, the way she was with the patients she followed. Follow is what we did, the students—get assigned patients and do little more than follow them along. It was the residents who did the real work, who picked up the patients, carried them. June was attentive to all of the violence in medicine and tried to talk her patients down when they moved toward agitation, aggression, or elopement. When scenes got tense, we were taught to leave and come back in numbers, get the residents, the men, the guards with their guns. This was called a show of force. But June, no matter what she encountered, always tried to defuse the situation herself. This was not, at heart, a belief that everyone could be reasonable but rather that everyone had their own kind of reason that could be, should be, brought to light. June and I would talk, sometimes, about the fear we felt in the face of hostile patients, or hostile doctors, or gushing blood, hypotension, cardiac arrest. A true even keel, we both supposed, must require some degree of indifference.

June always appeared to be single but alluded to what sounded like the affairs you read about in great literature: men, women, sometimes married, always much older than us. These entanglements never seemed sordid or financial, at least not the way I pictured them. The partners were just, in her telling, definitively unavailable. This is one approach to the problem of intimacy. For me, I always struggled just to find my feelings and tended instead to steal from my childhood friends, literally—their crushes, their boyfriends. Effort was always required. Whatever romantic interests I came up with on my own were always clearly inappropriate—the son of my sister's father, for example, or, somehow, not only my closest high-school friend but also her older sister, sort of at once, as a unit? The sister was a painter, and the friend remains one of the most coldly beautiful people I have ever met.

I do not remember whether I ever told her, but if I did, it was in a handwritten note. And if she responded, it was only a word: Don't.

So how I felt about June was a little vague to me until she started sleeping with the Texan. She told me, for some reason, everything about it, about how ungainly he was emotionally and how his back was covered in thick coarse hair, how he came too quickly and couldn't make her come at all. And I don't know what it made me want or who it made me feel sorry for. My only move was to stay up late with her drinking, stay too long in her apartment, sit beside her on the floor. Lean toward her, is all. It could have been anything. She dodged me, literally. Go home, she said. But she said it kindly.

No Apparent Distress

As the end of things circled around us, I kept waiting for Ada's husband to erupt with wisdom or clarity. He didn't. Maybe all the conflict with the staff—every specialist had another opinion, though in private they all agreed she would never leave the hospital—left him too spun and distracted for any dawning truth about the nature of love or anything. He looked more like someone who had survived the crash of an airplane, wrapped in a blanket, stunned and shaking.

I was learning something hard and fast that I had never known about love or marriage. But I won't know how to tell you what it was.

I saw my mother married once. She was working as a bank clerk and took a sick day for the wedding. The slaughterhouse man. I was ten and almost threw up when she told me. She was pregnant again. I had heard her a few weeks before on the telephone, crying, asking whoever what she should do. The wedding was just a judge and my mother's AA sponsor and that woman's husband and the groom. I wore the sponsor's daughter's shoes and an angel costume that was left over from a Christmas pageant. The slaughterhouse man was thin and menacing, but the baby was a girl, the first sister I ever had.

I had the only downstairs bedroom in the house, shared with some young brother. I would listen all night to the sounds of this stepfather after I was sent to sleep. Soon he began to pick fights with my mother about the food she cooked and the way she did the laundry. I would watch in the light through the door cracked open how he would hit her in the face and saw how he would push her, pregnant, shove her into a shelf and grab her when she fell to try and get the ring off her finger. A brother came down one night with a baseball bat. We were all tall children, but I can imagine this brother was scared. He never had to take a swing. I remember the sound of the rocks this stepfather threw against the car as we backed fast down the driveway.

The sister came out with a full head of hair. She had a constellation of birthmarks next to her nose and an easy smile and no lack of playthings. Or, at least, we treated her like a toy. The way we loved her seemed to bring some comfort to our mother, who was alone again with more kids than ever. This sister was still an infant when she moved into my room, and, later, older, she was the one I dragged out into the yard.

She was also the one to miss me most when I left. By the time she was twelve, she began to act out—smoking pot, cutting her arms with a box knife, sneaking boys into the house at night. Without much fanfare, my mother made plans to send her to a girls' home in some southern state where even the law is evangelical and called this saving her life. I imagined the place as though it were in the past, in the Dust Bowl, but in pictures my sister showed me after, it was just modern trash, particleboard and tar-paper lean-tos, sickly animals, the church run out of a farm shed made of corrugated steel. These fundamentalists were proud to beat their children. They had the parents sign waivers permitting corporal punishment.

The girls in one photo are lined up leaning on a bus, like prisoners, all in dirty thrift-store tees and long skirts made of denim. A lot of them were foster kids or failed adoptions, unwanted more than once. Above the garage, the pastor kept an apartment he would rotate the girls through; he'd come in at night and lay out his worries, his young kids, his unforgiving wife, then slide his hand up the girl's leg on the ratty sofa. Do you know how pretty you are? On Sundays they would sit at his feet and read the Bible.

My sister lived in that home for years, until the pastor's wife woke up one day and left, and the pastor fled shortly thereafter, fearing a legal reckoning that somehow never came. By then I was halfway through medical school. I had just finished obstetrics when she told me she was pregnant. She was living in another southern state, in the basement of another church. I had nightmares of her all alone, bleeding out or preeclamptic. But the baby was born without complication. Another little girl, another body susceptible to harm.

On the day that Ada's brain died, we had her daughter come in to say goodbye. Oh, the daughter kept a stone face for the child-life specialist we brought in to break the news. But when she came out of the little lunch-smelling conference room, she saw her father, and that was when she started screaming, and she didn't stop, and she screamed in a way that made the staff wonder if she might require sedation. I wanted to know how it felt to love someone so much. I can still see the bed as it was rolled from the unit, not with a nice white cinematic sheet outlining the shape of her body but with a blue square casing fitted to the bedrails so no one in the halls would dream that people died here. She had been silent for weeks before that day, and all the husband had wanted was one more conversation, one more exchange, even with the woman who faked remembering her breakfast.

That daughter. I sometimes want to call her on the phone. I don't suspect I will ever love anyone enough to feel that way when I have lost them. Or perhaps I mean that none of us will ever feel enough for anything. But it kills me, it breaks me down entirely, to see the world as full of backdated regrets when in real life we can seldom stand the sight of each other and work so hard to keep anyone from guessing what we need or feel. No one, for example, calls me. So when my phone rings, and it is family, I lose a breath and fear the worst—a fall, a death—fear it so badly that I almost believe that I want it by now: a death, a fall, something to freeze them all in time so I can come to terms with them.

And then some days I wonder, how could it matter? It is all just a thing that has happened.

Complicated Grief

I assisted at an abortion clinic one weekend during gynecology. First there was a girl unbearably young, crying silently, speechless, holding hands with an older sister. In the end they wanted time to think. Then an older woman with a few kids already. She was frank and ready to go. The machine that sucks the pieces out is large and loud. A new fellow was training. He spread the woman's legs and began gently, but the best way through is to get it over with fast. I held the woman's hand while she screamed and screamed.

Here is what I didn't know: We count the pieces after. A bin off the machine holds all the fetal tissue—we say *products of conception* for a neutral moral tone. And we take the bin into a back room and empty it into a square glass casserole dish over a lighted panel and use streams of saline and tweezers to pull the clumps apart until the pieces are recognizable as hips and legs and arms. The bones are almost clear, ghostlike in the shredded tissue. The fingers and toes are round impossible nubs. The eyes are there, far apart. The skull is in pieces. After some time, we account for it all.

Toward graduation, the Texan started sending me, instead of pornography, articles concerning fast fixes for existential distress: sensory deprivation, microdosed LSD, ketogenic diets. He said he wanted to help with my perpetual dread; this is called projection. I have found that the best way to handle fear is to call it up, bring it on, and try to outdo it. So I've been imagining explosions on the subway, the smoke all around, the strangers slipping into panic, my own heroic role. Maybe the world ends. I will be brave, I think. Well, everyone probably thinks that.

We lost one that last year, a classmate. He drowned, unclearly an accident. In this case, more than when someone has left a note, we could lean toward unbridled reverence. He was not a well-known figure. The memorial featured some photographs: him in a backpack, vaguely smiling. We were quick to accept we would never know what happened. Thoughts and prayers, that kind of thing. Half of us, at least, were chronically, passively suicidal, trudging on in what we could only guess was his same condition. It was so easy to imagine the memorials they would put up, for the woman in the army, say, or for any one of us wiped out in a plague, a catastrophe. They would run out of conference rooms to name for the deceased.

One day the Texan sent me a self-deception survey. It was written like a quiz in a teen magazine, but the content was all scatological, sexual, or morbid: Have you ever enjoyed your bowel movements? Do you ever feel attracted to people of the same sex? Have you ever felt like you wanted someone dead? I scored almost off the chart, the most honest score you could get. But the point, as it turned out, is that lying to yourself is the better way to live—it reduces stress, promotes dignity and resilience, and makes you better at competitive swimming. So much for introspection.

Esteban does not eat meat, nothing that had eyes, he says. Nothing with a mother. Which is fine—why kill anything you don't have to? But he likes the zoo more than anyone I know who isn't a child. Once we saw lions, right there in the city, on a cold day in autumn, practicing their roars. By their size and short weird manes, we guessed they were adolescents. The sounds they made were like the keening of cows, and we laughed at them, then laughed to laugh at something that could destroy us. He called them all people, called their front paws hands.

It was hard, though, to see the primates. Once there was a baboon right up against the glass. She had an old look and a gnarled tooth hanging out of her mouth, and you could go right up to her, just two inches of glass between your face and hers. And she just stared, delirious, deranged, with the blank, slow, searching look I know now from meeting the actively dying. I wanted to stay forever. I wanted to go in, really, and hold her or take her to a nice back room and wrap her up in blankets. Instead, I took a picture of her with my phone. To remember, I hope. I've never shown it to anyone.

And it's the same with the gorillas and orangutans. To be near them is a privilege but it can't be right at all. I heard a story once about a caged orangutan who learned to pick locks, so the people took away the wire he picked with, but he found another one and learned to hide it under his lip. And in the night, he'd let himself out, but all he ever did was go sit on top of the elephant house. To watch the sun rise, I guess. We tend to rank other animals by intelligence, which means according to how much they are like us. But who is like us—what are we like? How amazing we all are, and capable of any cruelty. A whale in captivity learned to imitate human speech. Not to say words but to spout a funny stream of urgent low-pitched gibberish. And crows make sleds from garbage to slide down snowy roofs.

At work I like the patients who are like me. No, not the women who come in battered already, who plead for themselves in the fast and desperate way that means they can't be trusted. I like the ones who are smart and afraid—the worried well, I sometimes hear the doctors call them. Those are the ones I like to console. Because who hasn't felt her heart beat so hard in her throat that she knew it would choke her and felt a flood like acid rush from tongue to toes and gone to the emergency department for a CT scan because her hands went numb and sat and watched through an oxygen mask as all the real emergencies rolled by, the broken arm, the gunshot, the preterm delivery. We've all been there. Right?

For most of the four years we were in school, the Texan's mother was dying. He told me this somehow the moment we met. She was in remission then, and he showed me a picture of her hairless head, which was covered over in winding patterns of brown-red ink, a sort of crown, and she was smiling. He was younger than me but the oldest in his family, and he worried constantly about his sister, who was home with the mother, at the bedside. He could talk at great length without interruption. He often led by saying: I'm not going to lie.

It wasn't long until his mother was sick again, in a bad way, with nothing left to do but join a research study. She was a nurse, so she understood the hopelessness of early-phase trials. Often in the hospital I saw these folks recruited by doctors hiding hopelessness in the fact that they were not God. *I'm not God* was what they said, in a context always meaning they couldn't say that a treatment would not work even when it was in a phase meant mostly to determine if the drug would kill a person. Its toxicity, I mean. But his mother knew this, and did it, and died.

She had been a nurse in rehab first and later at a hospice. She had a bad habit of bringing sad cases home. The worst one, John—though they were all named John—was dealing drugs from the house and hiding the profits in the walls. He stayed out for days once in the desert and got so close to coming back that he died of exposure or an overdose right on their porch. Oh God, I said when the Texan told me. We were at the bar where we always were, warming up for an exam on the Krebs cycle or something. Wait, he said. It gets better. After she found him and before the police arrived, she stripped us down and sent us to the boiling attic to dig through the unfinished walls and find his cash and hide it somewhere better. The picture it made, he said. Can you see it? The glistening kids pulling drug money from the walls.

One night after an exam, I went drinking with just the Texan. We got back to that dorm, the bare rooms, the cold linoleum. I had just barely passed, and he got a near-perfect score, and when we reached his floor he ran out of the elevator and began to take running leaps, running and jumping, punching at the glass domes that covered the overhead lights, yelling like a lunatic. Finally, one of them shattered, falling in shards and a cloud of white dust. His hand was bleeding. Let's get you inside, I said. I tried to coax him into his room. He started to shake and cry. He said, No, we can't, we can't. He said, We have to tell them. We have to tell them before they find out.

Can you see it? He laughed when he told me about being a kid in the attic with the dead man on the porch. Because what else do you do? I laughed. It was the worst thing I'd ever heard. And then my mother called me in the middle of the night. Sober for the moment, and all her children grown and gone. She said she had woken up newly afraid of the nothingness that was waiting, behind a car crash or a plane crash or a cancer already in place. Well, chest pain was how she described it. What do you do when it feels like that? she asked. And I thought of something I'd read somewhere: The world was made from nothing, and the nothingness shows through. But that's not what I told her.

Discharge Summary

When I first moved to the city, what struck me most were all the sounds that sounded like explosions. Fireworks, mostly. Backfiring cars. Alarms, of course, and sirens. I remember the tiles in the tunnel strobing white in the red brake lights as my bus came in. A small room, not much to unpack. By then I could set up anywhere and make it look like home. A poster from a French film, a certain blanket. And then just a whole life spread out in front of me.

Oh, there was a year between leaving home and leaving town. I am tempted to leave it out. My mother divorced me, legally. I could write my own sick notes for high school and went only four days a week and finished early on the honor roll. But something began to go wrong inside of me. My eyes, for example. Everything seemed blurry. Along the edges, at least, as though painted in a flat plane, without depth or perspective. The roads shifted as I drove, the curb a shock as a front tire bumped up onto it. I lived here and there. Once in a cluster of low-end town houses out past the highway, with hollow walls and hollow punched-in doors, and carpet in the hall that smelled like urine and mold. There was just one set of keys, and I didn't have it, so I followed other tenants through the main door and picked the second door's lock with my driver's license and slept on the floor.

The doctor's daughter was an infant when I left, and just a little after, in the deep midwinter, our mother had gone on a bender, and the baby wandered out onto the porch in nothing but a diaper. The police were called. She was blue and still when they found her, but alive, with all her toes and fingers miraculously intact. I went to see her a little after, and she screamed and screamed when she saw me, a stranger, and ran into the kitchen and hid behind the stove. That sister, the last one, is a teenager now. She just went on her first date. We talked and talked, she said. I told him everything, she said. I wanted to know what her everything was. She said she told him she had tried to kill herself when she was an infant. And she laughed as she told me this, in her voice a kind of pride. We are responsible, at least, for the stories we tell ourselves.

I have learned some skills in medical school that you might not expect. One is I am newly good at making phone calls. I used to sweat and shake before I could even order takeout. Now I can call any kind of place and demand information or well-timed appointments. And although I never knew the answers to the questions attendings loved to ask—the famous pimping that, true enough, can burn your sense of self-worth down to nothing—I was largely considered useful for my skill at finding things: old films, outside records, pillows, or lost false teeth.

Another skill is this: I am brave enough to ask people anything I want to know. So toward the end, on the phone, I asked my mother some questions. I asked how she had gotten through her life and what she made of it now. Through what? was how she answered. I asked about that night, the slaughterhouse man, the rocks. She said: I don't think about that kind of thing too much at all. And when I do, it's all just fractured. An image, a glimpse. She said she didn't need to play it on repeat. So it's my fault, in a way, for the way I see things, turn them over, bleed them for all they are worth.

When I finally left home, when I got to the city, there was something I needed that didn't exist. A paper, in print, that explained all the noises from the night before, and the smoke in a subway station, and the strange delays, and why a manhole cover happened to explode. Because something turns rotten when we stop having any answers. We forget to wonder when we forget to ask.

I never had money and always had cigarettes. At the stand on the corner, I could trade them for fruit. My face, I guess, had yet to lose that Midwestern openness. So people talked to me a lot, and I let them. The city is full of sad stories spoken like arguments, performed for cash. Or that's a crass way to say it. But I would meet the same man over and over, a man who said he was looking for a Western Union, that just down the block were his wife and kids and car, and could I help him out with a couple of bucks? I wanted him to stop. Because what was the money for, drugs? It wouldn't have bothered me at all. Not that I could pay him. But I wanted him to go ahead and tell me who he was.

I had a boyfriend then, a rich kid, a music student, and all this talking drove him up a wall. It's true it made it hard for me to get places, so I was late, always, and parted with any money I ever had. A woman in her fifties kept me in the park for hours, saying her partner had broken her jaw, had forced her to use methamphetamines. This was me just last year, she said. The picture she held up was beautiful and of her, I really do think, but peeling at the corners and with the soft sepia glow of a photo from the seventies. How can you take it? this boyfriend asked. So much lying. I had missed a date at the symphony. He needed me to know that she had done this to herself.

He was the one with the dead father, not Esteban. He watched the lights on the wall as the ambulance drove off with the body cold inside it.

The words in neurology all begin with *a-*, from the Greek that means *without*. *Aphasia*, without speech; *amnesia*, without memory; *agnosia*, without knowledge; *abulia*, without will. Every loss with its corresponding spot in the brain. Now they can see all this anatomy with functional imaging, but historically they learned it from patients with structural damage: tumors, strokes, penetrating head wounds.

One man with a massive glioblastoma had anosognosia—he couldn't understand that he was sick. The doctors wanted to know how to treat him, when to back off, how he wanted his last days to go. But when they tried to ask, he just laughed and laughed. I'm not dying, he kept telling them, any more than you are.

There are, too, people who fake their illnesses or purposely make themselves ill. If this is done to avoid, for example, paying a debt or going to prison, it is called malingering. If it is done for attention or to feel safe or be loved, it is called something else. This difference, in the literature, is called primary versus secondary gain. The former connotes manipulation, the latter mental illness. The difference between the two, from a legal perspective, like all intentions or objects of consciousness, is arbitrarily definitive.

That music student—he dropped out and we lost touch until a few years later when he briefly dated one of my classmates. She told me that on their first date, after more than a few drinks, he came on to her so forcefully that she felt she'd been assaulted. I wondered at first if this could be a misinterpretation and then wondered what it meant to wonder that. The worst part was, even after it happened, she still wanted him to *like* her. She wanted me to tell her how I had done it, how I had won his awful heart.

Around then, the end of college, I started to wonder if maybe light was God. Not as a joke, not really. We had just covered Einstein's special relativity. As you move closer and closer to light speed, you stretch out in length, and time slows down around you. And then, as close as you get, you can never really get there, because at that speed you explode, become energy, not yourself, not even matter anymore. Not anything. I brought this alt theology to office hours, but the physics professor was not impressed. None of this, he said, is a metaphor. I didn't tell him that lights had started to flicker whenever I walked under them. The low fluorescents in the corridors at school would flash and buzz above me in the empty halls.

Time of Death

Where did Ada go? Still there, still in bed, comatose, fluids that weren't tears in her eyes, like I told you. Every day her pupils flinched less and less to the lights I shined in them. And the husband, he never left. She had so many infections by then that special gowns had to be worn in her room at all times, and gloves, of course, then special soap to wash your hands once you left and took the gloves off. The husband said, I haven't showered in weeks. I must have a smell, he said, and he laughed like a child. You don't, I told him, and it was true. Weeks in there, sleeping in a chair, slumped toward the wall near the doorway. Couldn't we do better? In the ward where women go to give birth, which is in the children's hospital, they have large sofas that fold out into beds so that fathers can sleep soundly through protracted labor. So why this, for him, waiting out protracted death?

Once the doctors felt that there was nothing else to do, they really wanted Ada gone. Protracted death does not fit into the algorithm of intensive care. Live or die; shit or get off the pot. And she couldn't leave, and she couldn't live, so the various staff goaded her husband daily to let them take the tube out. The phrase they always used was *let nature take its course*. As if nature were something we all, at last, could choose to resort to.

To say it more plainly, every day for a week, staff came in, myself included, and tried to convince her husband to turn off the machines that kept Ada's body running. And he said, No, no, no. And it was his choice. At last he told me: This is just, what— one week, one month of your work? But I have to live here the rest of my life. Here without my wife, alone with this kid. And the choice I make? Tell them no. Tell them no forever. And tell them to leave us alone.

I'm sorry, I said. I meant it. And I did what he asked.

But the very next morning, her pupils were flat and still when I shined the light at them. I did it again and again as the husband watched from the corner. They're gone? he asked. Yes. I had told him what to expect.

I went to one of the fellows and told him about the pupils. It's hardly an emergency, he said, and made me wait through rounds. So I told the husband to go ahead and call the family, tell them to start making their long drives. And I dragged through the hours we reported on all the bodies lying silenced in their beds, silenced except for the rushes of breath from the ventilators, the melodic alarms: *help-me, help-me, I-cannot-breathe.*

There were three other patients I was following that day. One was a man with a history of attempting suicide who had hanged himself with a smuggled shoelace in the closet of a state-run sanatorium the day after he was admitted. His scans showed the great gray ribboning of diffuse anoxic brain injury, and even on sedatives he flinched spastically whenever he was touched. He had goals for end-of-life he had spelled out for his mother in advance, but she wouldn't let him off the hook that easily. In the end, the doctors placed tubes in his throat and gut and shipped him to a long-term facility to wait for death by infection. The other two patients were both young women who had been in perfect health until, after a day or two of fever or confusion, they started seizing and were now each in a medically induced coma. This is called NORSE— new-onset refractory status epilepticus. Some die in comas, some live with bum limbs or fractured intelligence, and some wake up one day as if it had all been a dream and ask: Where am I?

After rounds, after lunch, finally the fellow came. I asked if I could help perform the formal brain-death testing. I still don't know what that impulse was— protection? curiosity? We asked Ada's husband to step out, and closed the door. I filled a syringe with ice water from a Styrofoam cup and attached narrow tubing from a butterfly needle with the needle cut off. I laid a towel below her right ear, threaded the tube in, and pushed the plunger down as the fellow held her eyes open. In you or me, if we could stand to have it done, this test would produce in our heads an enormous sense of vertigo, and our eyes would beat from side to side to try to follow the world as it spun. Her eyes were still, though. I held them open while the fellow did the other ear. Her eyes were blue. I think they were blue. How could I forget?

For the last test, you pause the ventilator and see if the patient tries to take a breath without it. As you wait, you run blood gases and watch carbon dioxide build up until it hits a point where anyone should take a breath, just as a reflex. Oh, she did seem to move a little. Her chest didn't rise, but it sort of bucked. I looked at the fellow, who just shook his head.

In brain death, this is when the time is called. It was 2:32 p.m.

We started the vent again. They give families a brief but reasonable period of accommodation to gather at the bedside before the ventilator is shut off permanently. But in Ada's case, a mistake was made. A note was entered into the chart after the declaration of brain death that said her husband had signed consent to withdraw care. But he had not given his consent to this at all. He didn't even need to. Ada was brain-dead; the staff didn't need consent to turn off the machines. But I told three fellows that this was an error. I was inflamed on the husband's behalf: Tell them no. Tell them no forever. Listen, the night doctor said. The lady's dead. It doesn't matter. Stop acting like you're the doctor.

We all make mistakes when we are tired. I was tired. And so I left.

Ada, in the morning, was still breathing and still dead. None of the doctors had come to turn her off yet. And the family—well, a good half of them who had come in the night—had left. Her husband ran out to meet me in the hall. I needed to tell him he had to wash his hands. He was crying and crying. This is a nightmare, he said.

It was that bad note and a bad pass between the day staff and the night staff. In the paperwork, at night, Ada had come back to life. And a sister had been told that the husband had consented to have the tube pulled out and kill her. A fight ensued. She called him a killer and a liar and took the whole vigil, and the family left and drove home hours to someplace upstate. But that was the least of what he was crying about. Is she dead? Is she really dead? That was all he wanted to know now. Why was I the one who had to tell him?

So we took the tube out. I'm not a doctor, I said. The doctor in charge said that doctors didn't need to be there. I went in with a chaplain and a nurse from hospice and the respiratory therapist. We took all the tape off her face and hands, removed the tube, and wiped the tears from her eyes and the blood from her mouth. We undid all her straps and wires. We lowered the rails and set up chairs beside her. We picked up all the blankets and bowls and sheets and tubes and threw them into the trash. Then they came in, what family was left, and we all watched her heart die together.

Stay honest if you can, the husband said as I walked him to the elevator. I still don't know what he meant. I'll try, I said, and held him a little while he cried.

Holding Therapy

The end went the same way. No one had changed, and all of us had changed. Some had first or second children or came out as gay or got sober or lost faith or confessed an interest in family medicine. No big surprises, taken en masse. We had hoped, I think, a lot of us, for a starker transformation. We had wanted to somehow shed ourselves, to wake up in the end and find we were something bigger than we had been to start. The school shook gently in the wake of several belated reckonings. An anatomy professor was reprimanded for an old, unpunished practice of holding private lessons in his office where he drew organ systems on students' skin with lipstick. A lab tech was fired for selling the fingernails of cadavers for use in cosmetics tests. And there was a backlash against that psychiatrist, the one who got me in, for a book she had written decades ago that led to the deaths of several children in treatment for disordered behavior and insecure attachment.

Is this the direction we are moving in? A student asked this at a town hall in the main auditorium. A hospital administrator had just announced a large-scale cut in the training program for health maintenance and preventive medicine. That's not it, that's not what I would call it, he said. He was bald, and on his scalp were sunspot lesions we all knew the name of: actinic keratosis. He said no. He said, We are moving in no direction.

In the holding method, you take the child after she acts out or refuses to obey you, and while she remains withdrawn or insolent, you force her eyes open and wrap your arms around her, holding and holding until the moment is forced to catharsis. Reading it over, I thought of that William Carlos Williams story we read in our little seminar on soft skills, the one about restraining a kid to swab her throat for diphtheria. The language is bluntly resonant of sexual assault: *It was a pleasure to attack her. My face was burning with it.* The girl cried, *Stop it! Stop it! You're killing me!* I'm so bored with that reading, said the doctor running the seminar, a woman, an arts person, a consultant for a medical drama on television. All that political correctness. *Aren't you ashamed?* the mother yelled at the little girl restrained under a man's full weight. *Aren't you ashamed to act like that in front of the doctor?*

Here is how I lost it, I won't lie. One day in spring the sky turned green and the green leaves were torn off of all the trees, and a tornado tore down my Brooklyn street, and trees fell sideways with their roots upgrounded into iron fences, bending them like rubber. And another day the following summer, all the glasses on my shelves began to shake, and the frames on the walls swung in waves of swaying bedrock. I waited for the blast of the bomb it must have been, but it was only an earthquake. After that, my mother's house burned down—in fact, stayed standing but was hollowed out by fire. No one died, although anyone could have, any of those children, our mother herself. And then the lights all going on and off, all these signs pointing to nowhere. I started to wonder why none of it seemed to matter. All this had happened and would happen again, and worse things too, plagues and shootings and every sort of violence. I was tired of waiting. The cuts and burns were like marks on a map: You are here. The burns made little blisters that did their work for days.

I think of a patient who had been tasked with copying a cube. She just kept drawing parallel lines, then crossing them off like hash marks. Eventually, astonished, she put the pencil down. She said: I know this is wrong, but I can't do it any differently.

A theory about the neglected children, the ones who looked away from faces, who withdrew and barely spoke, the previously abused children or the children with autism or the international orphans who suddenly without reasonable preparedness were inserted into assorted American families, was that they needed safe restraint to thrash against, to rage and rage until they shed the horror of being so essentially abandoned. Holding therapy was also a tutorial for mothers who weren't well equipped, hereditarily, for the task—mothers who had not been held as children. The child was restrained in the arms of the mother, sitting in the mother's lap, face pressed against her chest. Larger children could be pinned, supine, with the mothers prone on top of them. In group holds, the mothers gained strength from each other, lying on the floor of a room filled with the cries of children. Some of the mothers were shouting too: I will not stop, I am in charge, I need you to want me.

Keep holding until he feels better.

Keep holding until you feel better too!

The therapy never killed anyone, but it inspired some threatening imitations. In one iteration, a simulation of rebirth, a girl of ten was held down wrapped in flannel sheets she was meant to fight her way out of. Instead, she asphyxiated.

In the realm of neglected children, a thought experiment. You take an infant—a girl, for some reason, in the published version—and raise her alone in a world set up so that she never sees color. White walls, white cups and spoons and furniture. She sees black, I guess, at night, and whatever color her body is, the parts of it that she can see. She is dressed in all white clothes. You take this child and teach her everything there is to know about light and refraction, about the rods and cones of the eye, every bit of color theory. I imagine she is precocious out of boredom and readily learns everything there is for her to know. But then, after all that, you show her a color, the real thing, you show her, say, the violent red of a poppy. And she learns something then, something different in character and magnitude from everything else she knew before. But how do you say what it is?

This exists, in every way, outside the bounds of the possible. Surely, for example, she would have seen red already—who could reach the age of reason never having seen blood?

To treat the fear of death, some recommend sitting in meditation beside a person who is dead already. In Thailand or somewhere they call this *holding hands,* or so I read in a men's magazine in the little room where I waited beside a white-noise machine for my turn in psychotherapy. What do you want from this? the therapist asked. I said, Unconditioned positive regard. But she didn't laugh. I have heard it is necessary, in psychology, to believe that a treatment will work. Necessary, but not sufficient. The article said that you hold hands to confront the ghost, or your fear of ghosts, or to terrify yourself into clarity or ego dissolution or death? It was a little unclear on the specifics. The author did not seem possessed of overwhelming depth. It takes, I imagine, some paucity of self-awareness to be a tourist in a place like that. Like the Texan. I can hear him already—Oh, I held it, the hand, it moved, I heard a rustling in the trees. He wouldn't want to stop telling somebody about it.

Distress Tolerance

Once I was sent to get blood from a man about a thousand years old. He was rolling with dementia, legs and knees like tent poles under the sheet. His skin was slick and shined with crystals produced by his failing kidneys. His veins were broad but slipped around under the skin, and every time I stuck him, he cried out, newly surprised that I'd come all this way just to hurt him. When I came back bloodless, the doctors sighed and sent me back with one of my peers. It was the country-house man, a few years since I'd last seen him up close. He got the blood after four or five deep attempts. What's the secret? I asked him. He said: I pretend they can't feel anything.

They made a prize for humanism and let the students bestow it on one another. The class president was a humanist, and the country-house man, and the Texan was a humanist, and the woman with all the guns.

I asked that poet, the Orthodox Jew who was going to be a brain surgeon, how it felt to get so near death as a child. He said it always felt normal, even though the news kept turning worse. He didn't know how to explain. He did remember worrying a lot about his family, about how sad his illness made them. I never thought that death would be the end, he said, until after I got better. Now he had nothing but an itch, a conviction that nothing we did with our human lives mattered much at all. He said, The best we can do is try not to see it.

It made me want to tell him something my mother once said, about how every building has its madman. I had been living in Brooklyn in a bare apartment in that Caribbean neighborhood, and one night a man set fire to my neighbor in the elevator. He wore coveralls, had filled a pump sprayer with kerosene. Then he went and set her apartment on fire, the unit below mine. He was hiding on the roof when we all ran out through the smoke. A policeman on the scene told me that the woman's burned body was the worst thing he'd ever seen in his life. Although the fire was minor and the man quickly arrested, I called my mother even though we rarely really speak. She said: Why are you worried? Now you have the safest house in the neighborhood.

Around the time her house burned down, my mother was underwater on pills she had bought off the internet. After the fire, she and what children were still at home moved into a motel and ate a continental breakfast every day for a year. And something happened to me too. I went out with a friend and had too much to drink, and then he did things to me while I was too sick to move. Our friends when I told them did not believe me, and then I didn't believe myself. Within days I could not remember what I had said, the timing or directness of my expressed dissent. I couldn't get the story straight at all. I described the whole thing, end to end, only once, to the therapist. She said, What do you want it to have been? So I never brought it up again.

How do you recover from anything? The cure, of course, is charitable works, said a teacher who spent her off-hours writing personal ads for dogs at the kill shelter. Also, she would take them out on the designated day, show them the green grass along the river, touch her head to their heads, tell them they were good—then return them to the place where they would be euthanized. Everyone else was telling me to protect myself. And what would happen if I did not?

If you live near an understaffed emergency department, they will let you dress in scrubs and hand out patients' meal trays and bring around warm blankets. They will let you fill the bins of lactated Ringer's and normal saline that temporize sepsis. Once you know where to find the sutures, the surgeon will let you stand behind him as he closes a man's hand, a hand that caught, between thumb and first finger, the ax his wife had aimed at his head. Once you find your way around the basement, you can bring up boxes of gauze and gloves, stay useful late into the night. And once you know the nurses well enough, you can do anything at all that interests you; you can wash and wrap the bodies that come in found down, the ones you are first allowed to practice compressions on.

In the end, in a way, you only have to pass calculus and physics, some basic science classes, and a large-scale standardized test to get a place in medical school, if you can find a way, of course, to pay for it. I taught English in the outer boroughs in the morning, took classes uptown at night. In my whole life before that, I had never known and never would have guessed what the thing I wanted looked like, something cold and clean and right: a stitched half-severed hand.

Don't worry about your weaknesses, was another thing that teacher said. Just take your strengths and play them to death.

Goals of Care

That little boat still stops by the bridge. I think this, although I haven't seen it since Ada died. I left the dorms and got a place with Esteban, two rooms now, with no view of bridge or river. Instead, our windows face a small park where people come with their dogs, and where their children have birthday parties with piñatas hung from the branches of the trees, and where dogs and children run through the little lawn until the grass bares down to dust. The lawn is all fenced off now, but only until the grass grows back. The little boat is part of the harbor patrol—a patient told me that, a former policeman. There is a watchman in the boat, watching for suspicious activity, for anyone who might come and try to blow something up.

I met Esteban after the fire, the assault, the hurricane.

He was not in seminary, not yet, but he was the handsomest man I had ever seen. And that was just when everything inside me fell apart. I started seeing things, feeling things, choking on thin air on the subway. For relief I cut small marks, in secret spots at first, but soon they were out in the open and clearly ticked up both my arms. We didn't know what to do with me. He took me to a doctor, and the doctor sent me in. But I washed my hair first and blew it out with a round brush. I put on my best clothes because I thought it would help.

They took my clothes and my shoes and left me in a white room where I was questioned for hours. What did they ask, and what did I tell them? About the lights, yes, the violence, the basement. That I was so afraid I could die. Looking back, I understand it was a medical student, a resident, and then an attending. To me then, it was an interrogation. A patient in the hallway shouted over and over, That's not a promise, it's a threat. He looked me, everyone, right in the eyes and said, Don't take anything they give you. What they gave me made my head tilt so far to the right that all I could do was lay it down. I tried to refuse when the pills came again but the nurse said if I wanted to leave, I'd better think hard before refusing anything. I stopped. Esteban came with cold coffee and magazines. I cried and he would try to sit next to me. Don't do that, the guard would shout. He really did have a gun.

When I did get out, a little before my seventy-two hours were up, since Esteban really did run a small doctor down in the halls, he was nowhere to be found. So I collected my things from some kind of desk, along with a receipt for the pocket change that had been in my pants, and walked out alone through that glass house and went to a deli for cigarettes. The nurse really said: Don't ever come back here again.

And I didn't come back—or I did, but only once—until the day I showed up for that interview.

To get over what you've come from but to stay who you are—what would that even look like? I listen at night sometimes while Esteban prays quietly aloud, most often just a list of names. Mine, my mother's, all of the brothers and sisters, his family, his patients. Some of mine. All lists are beautiful, I think, as with attention, they take on a cadence that sounds like the songs we must have sung before we could speak, as just monkeys in the trees. I pray too, but only as a joke: Bless this Thai food, which we hath received from thy bounty.

Now Esteban is working as a chaplain in the hospital. He carries a pager that sounds whenever someone is pronounced dead. He comforts the grieving, holds them, or prays, or at least keeps the mothers from hitting their heads on the walls or the floor. The worst, he says, are the perinatal losses. There is nothing to hold on to when a newborn dies, nothing to reflect on or be grateful for. He calls this a pure void of grief. Other times his job is just to stay with the body, because some religions prohibit leaving dead bodies unattended. I always feel bad for the body. The ribs really break. You come to hate the sound of it. So he sits with dead bodies and prays what he prays until the rabbi or whoever comes to take over. It seems right to me. The doctors stream out fast after death is called, leaving a wake of plastic wrappers and papers and tubes and empty saline pushes. Esteban says that sums up all his work in a way: staying with the body.

I join Esteban in church, though not often. There are parts I like, the colored glass, the bells, the confessions: Forgive us for the evil that we have done and for the evil that is done on our behalf. But the baptisms destroy me. I am destroyed and come back together. So I prefer the little church that is hidden in the hospital, where the services are rare enough to easily avoid. Weeks or months now since Ada died, and almost graduation. The entrance to the chapel is hard to find, industrial-looking, like a service exit. And then a little hall to larger doors, softened in old leather. A man in scrubs sits silently to rest or maybe pray. A couple in coats talk softly in a corner. The only word I hear at all is *terrible*. A woman in a white coat silences a sudden sound from a pager. An old man in a driving hat takes a seat by the altar, leans over, and ties his shoes.

But I lied about the windows when I said they were boarded up from behind. There are no boards. On three walls outside, there is a garden. And light shines through the rose window, making it a muted kaleidoscope, orange and blood red and yellow, that one deep blue you see only in shining stones. It shines most along the long wall, the colors dark and glowing. The dark room is always warm. There are menorahs now on the edges of the inlet where a priest would prepare a sacrament. Muslims pray here, too, toward

Mecca, which is a place in the world somewhere in the direction of the rose window. It must always be dark in this room; it must always hold the old smoke of incense and old robes. And what am I doing here? It is hard to know. Still, it looks like nowhere else in the hospital.

Acknowledgments

Deepest thanks to those whose support made this work possible: Stephen Douglas, Garielle Lutz, Sarah Burnes, Sophie Pugh-Sellers, Vivian Lee, Louisa McCullough, Jayne Yaffe Kemp, Tracy Roe, Rita Charon, Amy Hempel, Jenny Offill, Peter Chamberlin, Ruth McCann, Amit Suneja, Joe Tobias, Giselle Jaconia, Laura Kolbe, Daniel Gallo, Aimee Davidson, Nicholas DeForest, Catherine Varner, and many others, alive and dead, whose names I cannot mention.

About the Author

Anna DeForest is a neurologist and palliative care physician in New York City. Her writing has appeared in the *Alaska Quarterly Review,* the *Journal of the American Medical Association,* the *New England Journal of Medicine,* and the *Paris Review.* This is her first novel.